To Track A Copycat

To Track A Copycat

by Marian Weston

ORC PRESS

Copyright © 1995 by Marian Weston
Library of Congress Cataloging
in Publication Data:
Weston, Marian
To Track A Copycat

95-068519
ISBN   1-882270-34-7

No part of this book may be reproduced
or utilized in any form or by any means.
Published in the United States of America
by ORC Press.
Inquiries should be addressed to:
Editor: ORC Press
1495 Alpharetta Highway, Suite I
Alpharetta, Georgia 30201

Contents

Chapter 1	1
Chapter 2	25
Chapter 3	47
Chapter 4	66
Chapter 5	85
Chapter 6	110
Chapter 7	124
Chapter 8	149
Chapter 9	164
Chapter 10	183

Chapter 1

Kay checked her watch.

Forty-five minutes had elapsed already and no one had claimed her. She didn't expect the keys to the city, but if this was the way the Eye Clinic greeted its volunteers, she was beginning to question the wisdom of coming at all. Hers was the last plane arriving from the States to Haiti.

The crowds were gone. The Customs officials had closed up their gates. There wasn't even anyone at the Reservation Desk. It was as if the day itself had been cancelled.

There were no planes landing here at Port-au-Prince, so where was the official greeter?

Even if she were standing in the wrong place, she'd expect that the Information Desk at an airport terminal would be the best place to wait. She was quite visible to anyone, since there weren't any other tourists around. She had no idea how far she was from the clinic. Still, if she weren't picked up soon, she'd take a cab.

Out of the corner of her eye she saw the biker, hunched well over the handlebars, coming right towards her. Why would anyone ride a bike inside a terminal?

As he sped closer she recoiled, distancing herself from the impending disaster. He leaned over and with a wide swoop scooped up the two suitcases next to her and rode off.

Two suitcases? She only came with one. The other belongs to whom? But he took mine and that's what counts.

"Hey," she yelled, springing to life. She ran after him as best as she could in her three-inch heels, then stopped momentarily, bent down, and removed her shoes. Now she could fly.

But outside the terminal the biker was nowhere to be seen. She squinted in the distance. Who knows in what direction he went.

Whatever was she going to do? Her luggage was gone. What a mess! Nobody around to talk to, to report the loss, nothing. Hopeless situation.

How could this happen to her, in Haiti, of all places? This was supposed to be a lovely island with pleasant people, she had been told. Robbing tourists simply didn't occur here. Well, she'd have to do something to spark action. The police. She reentered the terminal building and headed for a phone just as a tall, solidly built man in khaki washpants and pale yellow sport shirt dashed towards her.

"Kay Thompson? Let's go." Kay didn't get a chance to acknowledge her name or ask him who he was.

"Hurry," he yelled at her.

Follow him? What if this guy is in cahoots with the thief?

"We'll get him. Come on. Don't stand there. Move." He motioned to the jeep parked nearby.

"I'm Dr. MacDonald from the clinic and I was afraid something like this would happen if I didn't get to the airport early. Unfortunately, I got tied up at the clinic."

Kay just nodded, not comprehending, bewildered at the sequence of events that tumbled around her, catching her in their wake. "He took my luggage," she managed to say.

"I know. I know. Don't worry. We'll get him."

"How do you know in what direction he went?" she asked.

"He always returns home with his loot, then sorts out the stuff he wants to sell. He has been warned about his thievery in the past and still hasn't learned his lesson, but he won't get far with all the luggage."

"There he is, look, straight ahead, hang on." The jeep bounced wildly. MacDonald pulled in front of the biker, braking jerkily to a stop, blocking his way. He dashed over to the culprit.

"Man, please, Man, let me keep it this time, just this once."

"No," Dr. MacDonald was saying. "You can't take something that doesn't belong to you. The lady needs her luggage." And with that, he wrenched first one suitcase and then the other from the thief's grasp, and rejoined Kay in the jeep. He placed the small case between them and stowed the larger one in the back.

"Aren't you going to call the police?" Kay asked.

"What for? The guy's harmless. Besides, the police will only complicate my own life right now."

Kay scrutinized the small attache case wedged between them. "Doctor, this isn't mine."

"I know," Dr. MacDonald said. "That's for me. A Customs official had called me to let me know it had arrived. Now that we got that settled, I hope you don't think this is going to be a romantic holiday."

Was he kidding? "I'm here to work at the clinic," Kay said matter-of-factly.

"Glad you told me. I wouldn't have known."

"I assumed you were informed by my school that I was going to be a volunteer," Kay said.

"Oh, we were informed, all right, but I don't think we're quite prepared for a beautiful green eyed blonde dressed to kill."

"I'm sorry if I don't measure up to your specifications."

If only Jim Barlow had met me, Kay thought, as the official

greeter. Mary Ellen said her fiancé was kind of an optometric extern here. Then I wouldn't have to go through this inquisition.

"How wonderful that you've got me all figured out already, Doctor."

"The clinic always seems to attract sweet young things, eager to save humanity. From what, I don't know."

"And I certainly didn't expect a reception like this."

"What did you want? The full red carpet treatment with a twenty-one-gun salute and an entourage from Duvalier's palace? You do know who Duvalier is, don't you?"

He chided himself. Why are you baiting her? You just met her. She has done nothing wrong and most likely, she came here with the purest of motives. He stole a glance at her. She's a stunner. Maybe I'm afraid for her, he thought. Afraid she might lose that idealism.

"I'm glad to hear you aren't expecting some kind of an exotic adventure," he said at length.

Kay glared at him.

"This is a very poor country," the doctor continued. "We try, in our own small way, to brighten the life of the average Haitian with a pair of glasses."

"I see," said Kay, trying hard to control the resentment mounting within her.

"We'll stop at the hotel first and get you a room and then proceed to the clinic."

"Where do the volunteers stay?"

"Not in a luxurious villa, *mademoiselle*."

What was the use of asking him anything? His artless replies only served to heighten the growing friction between them.

"As you know, the clinic and school share the cost," he said. "That is, we try to. We're going to have to do something to ease up on the financial burden one of these days. One thing our hotel can boast about, though, is an authentic French chef."

"Our hotel?" Kay asked.

"We all stay at one place. Does that bother you?"

"Of course not. Why should it?"

"It's easier to keep tabs on the volunteers that way."

Curiously, Kay watched him as he spoke. His shock of thick black hair was flecked with gray. The square jaw signalled an authority that would brook no interference.

Ahead of them now, like a mirage rising from the sea, was a two-storied creamy, stucco building. Shrubs of pink oleander fringed the periphery of the walk leading up to the entrance. A line of Royal palms, visible from the front, defined the perimeter of a formal garden in the rear of the building.

"Here we are," the doctor said, parking the jeep. He carried her luggage and the attaché case into the hotel, preceding her and holding the door open for her. The small lobby contained nondescript rattan furniture and the ubiquitous ceiling fan. The doctor walked with Kay to the front desk.

"This is a new student volunteer for the clinic," he said to the clerk behind the desk. "What rooms do you have available?"

The clerk smiled hospitably at Kay and she reflected that this was the first decent welcome she had received so far.

"Only six and nineteen are left."

The doctor thought for a moment. "Six has the bath, hasn't it?"

The clerk nodded.

"Give her Number Six then."

As Kay walked toward a nearby flight of stairs, she heard Dr. MacDonald inquire, "Is that new bellboy around? Michel is his name, right? When he has a chance, have him slip this in my room. I left my key at the clinic."

Kay saw MacDonald hand the attaché case over to the desk clerk. "Tell Michel to put this in my closet," the doctor said.

He turned to Kay. "I think you'll appreciate Number

Six. It has its own shower, but no air conditioning and no balcony."

Kay said nothing. She would have liked to slip off the beige and white striped shirtwaist she was wearing and freshen up.

"There are only three rooms with private baths," the doctor explained. "The rest of us have to share a bathroom down the hall." He gave her the key to her room and picked up her luggage. "Follow me."

They climbed a circular mahogany staircase, its balustrade of wrought iron, that led to the upper floor. Kay inserted the key into Number Six and Dr. MacDonald placed the suitcase inside.

The furnishings were adequate but Spartan. A large teakwood table served as a writing desk, mismatched with a chair of cane in the center of the room. A hurricane lamp perched on the edge of the desk. A small woven rug of sisal on the floor appeared as an afterthought, since it barely covered anything.

On the wall was a Haitian primitive depicting women at the marketplace. The bathroom was tiny, but the stall shower was going to be a luxury Kay knew she'd enjoy.

"These louvered shutters," Dr. MacDonald was saying as he demonstrated for her, "can be opened like this to give you lots of fresh air." The brass frame of the bed caught the glint of the sun's rays then. "Should we go?" he said impatiently. "I'll take you over to the clinic and then you can meet Ruth Emerson, our R.N., and she'll show you around."

Now the jeep plowed through forests of trees heavy with crimson blooms. Kay couldn't fail to see, amid the lush mantle, the one-room homes of thatched mud and concrete block standing in stark relief against leafy green mango and breadfruit trees.

"Do you know anything about the clinic and the kind of work it has been doing?" Dr. MacDonald asked suddenly.

"Not too much, really."

"Didn't your school tell you anything?"

"Only what was on the bulletin board."

"Weren't you sufficiently interested to know what else was involved?" The disapproval in his voice was mirrored in his eyes as he glanced briefly at her.

"I was interested, but I assumed that the material I read was all there was to it."

"Good God, girl, did you think this was going to be a picnic?"

"Dr. MacDonald, would you mind not calling me 'girl'?"

"Why not? You sure look like one." He arched a brow, then chuckled.

"My name is Kay and I expect to be addressed like that," she said, exasperated with him.

"You'll find, young lady, that you can't get high and mighty on this job, in case you have any ideas. Come to think of it, when we get through working you six days a week, you'll be too tired to have ideas," he paused, "about anything."

He had his nerve talking to her like that. His rudeness was insufferable. She came to Haiti with only one desire: to help people at the clinic. It was difficult to brush aside the increased sense of discomfort that his antagonism caused and this was only her first day, she reflected gloomily.

Dr. MacDonald remained tight-lipped after that exchange and concentrated on the driving. Kay also kept her gaze straight ahead, especially when she noticed there were no guard rails to keep anyone safely hemmed in on the narrow road. Below them was a craggy abyss, stretching well beyond her vision.

Another turn in the road brought them to the clinic, a one-storied, rambling structure of white stucco with a low pitched roof, set back a ways from the road.

"It's quite large," Kay said.

The doctor laughed. "What did you expect, a tent like the Big Top?"

Kay felt her cheeks grow warm.

"Didn't you ever see a picture of the clinic?" he asked.

"No."

"Once you get inside, you'll see how cramped we are in space. We need more space, more volunteers, more money for supplies. Everything."

Dr. McDonald parked the jeep, ushered Kay into the clinic, and presented her to Ruth Emerson, a tall willowy brunette who assessed Kay from top to bottom but otherwise was friendly. Ruth was in charge of student assignments and conducted Kay on a tour of the facilities.

"We do everything here except fit contacts," Ruth said, grinning. "We usually get several students together, but today you were the only one deplaning." Ruth squeezed Kay's arm. "We're happy to have you aboard because we sure could use an extra pair of hands to take some of the routine duties away from the doctors, who are horribly overworked."

In every room there were Haitians standing in line. Young people, mothers with babies and small children, old people. "Must be a hundred people waiting," Kay observed.

"More like hundreds," Ruth said, smiling. "They're a very patient people. They wait resignedly and without complaints, regardless of how long. Some have been awaiting their turn for a couple of days."

Ruth didn't even get a chance to introduce Kay to Jim Barlow when he rushed forward to grasp her hand. "Mary Ellen wrote me you'd be here. It's great having someone from home."

"You know him?" Ruth asked as they moved on.

"Not exactly. He's the fiancé of my best friend and she told me he was at the Eye Clinic."

There was another optometric student, a couple of optometrists, and some Haitian nurses and aides Kay met before Ruth led her back to their starting point.

"And here's where you'll be working," Ruth said. "The doctor you've been assigned to is our ophthalmologist, the only M.D. we have at the present, Dr. MacDonald."

Kay grimaced. The idea of being bossed by MacDonald the next few weeks intensified a growing apprehension she was afraid to face in the first place. Why was it her misfortune to be thrown in with an older man who was always rancorous towards her. First it was Uncle Ted, then Biff, and now this physician."

"You don't look too happy about that," Ruth observed.

"I guess I'm kind of tired from the flight."

"Why don't you sit and watch me for awhile? You'll be following the same routine. Then if you have any questions about the procedure, I'll brief you."

The first patient who came to Ruth was wearing his glasses halfway down his nose. He gestured, sliding a finger up and down his nose.

"An adjustment. That's easy," Ruth said, winking at Kay.

When the patient left, Kay asked, "Do you speak the language?"

"No," Ruth said, "but it wasn't too hard to figure out that problem."

Dr. MacDonald came down the hall with a patient he had examined. "Ruth," he said, "see what you can do about filling this prescription."

He barely gave Kay a glance. Kay watched him walk back to his office with another patient.

"Kay," Ruth said, "if you want to hop over a little closer, I'll show you how we do this. We try to find a pair of glasses as close as possible to what's in our inventory here. Sometimes that's difficult because the one lens might be what we're looking for, but the other lens might not."

"So what do you do then?" Kay asked.

"Punt." Ruth grinned. "If you have any questions, talk to Mac. He'll be more than happy to help you."

Oh sure he will, thought Kay, so he can prove to himself how inept I am. No thanks.

Kay noticed that Ruth verified the prescription through the lens meter even though it was written on a tag attached to the glasses.

"Where did you get your optical training?" Kay asked.

"On the job, you might say, and Dr. Mac was helpful. We didn't have anyone to fill in and I was suddenly elected."

"Do you use your nurse's background at all?"

"Lots of opportunities here: wounds, lacerations. Excuse me for a minute, Kay. Sit, sit here," Ruth said, motioning to a patient who was holding what looked like a dirty rag over his right eye.

"Here's where I put on my nurse's cap," Ruth said. "First, we have to get rid of that dirty rag. This is probably a foreign body." Kay watched her take a cotton applicator and then turn the upper lid inside out by rolling it around the stick.

"There it is," Ruth said triumphantly. She took another cotton applicator and this time wiped the foreign body from underneath the lid. A broad smile on the face of the patient was her reward. "Now for some antibiotic ointment in the eye and he'll be as good as new."

"Is that something I'll have to do, too?" Kay asked.

"No. If you get a patient with something in his eye, just turn him over to Mac. Think you can take over tomorrow?"

"I'm sure I can," Kay said confidently.

"Don't forget, if you have any questions at all, ask Mac."

Kay remained silent.

"He expects you to ask questions," Ruth said. "Kay, even though you've had the formal training, you'll soon realize that experience in the real world is almost unrelated to what you learned in the classroom, especially in this situation. Time to wrap up things," she said. "There's Dr. Mac now. Dr. Mac, could you take Kay back to the hotel while I finish some paperwork?"

"Might as well," he said, looking directly at Kay. "I'm through for the day."

As they headed back to the hotel Dr. MacDonald said, "I suggest that when you report to work tomorrow, go easy on the eye makeup. We're not interested in the glamour bit."

Kay bristled, but said nothing.

They drove in silence then until the jeep stopped in front of the hotel.

Kay placed her hand on the door handle.

Dr. MacDonald studied her. "One other thing, get rid of the earrings when you come to work."

Kay turned to face him. "Dr. MacDonald, I didn't know there was a dress code on this job."

"There ought to be," he said, eyeing her coolly.

"Let me tell you something, Doctor. I just got off the plane. I have no more intention of wearing clothes like these to work than wearing a bikini."

He smiled at her outburst. "Simmer down. Save all that energy for the clinic. You'll need it. We've got lots of work to do."

"Anything else?" Kay asked.

"I wouldn't go traipsing around in three-inch heels, either. Not too practical. One final item. I'll be waiting for you in the lobby tomorrow morning at 8:00 o'clock sharp, so be ready. I don't like to wait for females who take forever, primping in front of a mirror."

Kay slammed the door of the jeep, as if in defiance of that demand. She was tempted to head for the airport that moment and fly straight home. Then she'd go back to her school and tell the real story of being a volunteer here. Of course, she wouldn't be hurting him, only the innocent people she saw waiting today, the people that required and needed medical attention.

In her room, Kay removed the three narrow spiraled bangles that dangled from her wrist and the matching earclips of titanium. She showered leisurely, feeling more relaxed, then dressed in a softly gathered broadcloth skirt of cranberry, matched with a blouse of lighter hue and a cummerbund of dove grey that nipped in her waist, and went downstairs into the dining room for dinner.

The waiter was quite solicitous, recommending some Creole specialties of the house: guinea hen with sour orange sauce, rice and black mushrooms, served with a sauce of onions and herbs.

Kay ate slowly, thoroughly savoring the food, unwinding in spite of everything. The sound of a woman's laughter arrested her attention. She saw Ruth Emerson dining with Dr. MacDonald four tables away. Ruth's hand rested easily on his arm as she leaned intimately towards him.

Kay averted her gaze. No sense in ruining her appetite for the delicious meal before her. The waiter removed the dinner dishes and brought her the dessert of sweet potato pudding and mango pie. A cup of strong Haitian coffee was served alongside. Kay looked up momentarily and caught Ruth's eye. Ruth smiled and tapped Dr. MacDonald's arm and he stared at Kay, not a smile of recognition on his face. Ruth walked over to Kay's table.

"Have an after dinner drink with us when you're through with your meal," she invited.

Kay was reluctant. She didn't relish the idea of being peered at by Dr. MacDonald or having to continue to fence with him.

"Come on," prodded Ruth. "It will give us a chance to get better acquainted. Don't be shy," she said, observing the hesitancy.

It wasn't shyness that made Kay hesitate. Instead, she was trying to think of some kind of an excuse that would get her off the hook so she wouldn't have to accept the invitation.

She was not interested in becoming better acquainted with a man like Dr. MacDonald; but how could she say that to Ruth. Kay didn't like him: his arrogance, his chauvinism, his cavalier treatment of her. The less she had to do with him after hours, the better she liked it. It was bad enough she'd be working with him on a daily basis.

"Still haven't decided to join us?" Ruth asked, watching her.

"I'm sorry," Kay replied, embarrassed. "I guess I'm more fatigued than I realized. Jet lag, I suppose."

"Come on over, anyway," Ruth said. "A good drink will rejuvenate you." With that, she returned to her table. Kay noted that when Ruth sat down, she whispered something to Dr. MacDonald, who glanced briefly in Kay's direction, and nodded.

• • • •

Kay finished her dessert and reasoned that she might as well be pleasant towards Ruth. After all, Ruth did extend a hand in friendship and there was really no need for her to create any more tensions on the job than necessary, especially, when they were all working towards the same goal: better eye care for the Haitians.

She rose slowly from her chair and walked over to where Ruth and Dr. MacDonald were seated.

"Congratulations! You finally made it over here," said Dr. MacDonald.

Kay glared at him.

"Mac, cut it out," Ruth said, hitting him playfully on the wrist. "Have a seat, Kay," Ruth said hospitably. "That's a stunning outfit you're wearing."

"Thank you," Kay said, noticing that Ruth was wearing a dirndl splashed with large sunflowers, teamed with a low-necked, puffed sleeve peasant blouse.

"Did they feed you enough tonight, Miss Thompson?"

He was bent on provoking her for no apparent reason. How she wanted to lash out at him; but what would be the point of it. She'd accomplish nothing but hard feelings all around. "Yes," she said at last.

"Kay, what would you like to drink?" Ruth asked.

"Whoa, Ruth, hold on," Dr. MacDonald interrupted, "this kid isn't old enough."

"Dr. MacDonald," Kay began, trying hard to keep her anger from surfacing, "I'm not a kid. I happen to be twenty-six and am quite old enough to drink, thank you."

"Serves you right, Ian," Ruth said. "Consider yourself having been told off."

"Must have been those freckles that threw me off."

Kay and Ruth ordered Tia Marias. The doctor had a Scotch and soda, then leaned back in his chair and continued his silent scrutiny of Kay.

"You're really a long way from home, aren't you?" Ruth asked.

"All the way from Iowa." Kay flashed her a smile.

"Did you earn a degree?" Ruth asked.

"Only a certificate indicating completion of study."

"What specifically did you study?" Ruth asked.

"I learned about frame selection and the art of cosmesis, matching a style with the shape of one's face."

"That won't help much out here," Dr. MacDonald said dryly. "Didn't you study any hard-core academic subjects?"

"The anatomy and physiology of the eye, and optics." Kay saw the smirk on Dr. MacDonald's face. She controlled the urge to slap him.

"That qualifies you to do what? Perform cataract surgery?" he asked, chuckling.

"I never said it did," Kay hotly denied.

"Kay," Ruth said, "I see you've had some modeling experience. No wonder you wear your clothes so well."

Kay smiled.

"Whatever possessed you to put that down on your resume?" Dr. MacDonald asked.

"I felt that my experience with people would enhance my potential as an optician."

"As a model?' Mac said. "Now I've heard everything."

"I understand what Kay is saying," Ruth said gently.

"Then you're the only one. Modeling experience here is about as useful as raising llamas."

"Kay," Ruth interceded, "what do you plan to do with your training when you're through in Haiti?"

"I'll probably work for an optometrist."

"Not an ophthalmologist?" Dr. MacDonald asked, grinning at her.

"Working here," Kay began, "will . . ."

"Cure you of that," Dr. MacDonald interrupted.

"Mac, for Pete's sake, let her finish," Ruth said. "As you were saying, Kay . . ."

"I think the doctor has already said it."

"Touché, Mac," Ruth said, tweaking him under the chin.

A three piece ensemble which had been playing during the dinner hour was now joined by a drummer and the vibrations of the goatskin drums beat out the sensuous rhythm of the meringué.

"Would you like to dance?" Dr. MacDonald asked, looking directly at Kay.

"Go ahead," Ruth urged. "I'll take my turn afterwards."

Dr. MacDonald rose and escorted Kay out on the dance floor. He slipped one arm around Kay's waist and held her close. Kay tensed for a moment when the pressure of his fingers brought her even closer. "Just relax," he said, "and concentrate on swiveling those hips. I'll do the rest."

They danced in silence and the doctor seemed unusually grim. Kay had to admit he was an excellent dancer. She was effortlessly doing intricate steps she had never done before as he led her expertly across the floor. The music stopped and they walked back to their table.

"Ruth, it's your turn," Dr. MacDonald said. "Sounds like a disco number."

Kay watched them as they danced. Dr. MacDonald became an entirely different person with Ruth, laughing and talking quite volubly. The metamorphosis in the man was apparent. Ruth was laughing, too, and enjoying herself. When the music ended, Ruth linked her arm possessively through the doctor's.

"That was fun," she said, plopping down in her chair. "Do you like to dance, Kay?"

"I always did."

"Until tonight, is that it?" Dr. MacDonald said.

"Ian, give her a chance to answer," Ruth said.

"If you'll excuse me," Kay said, "I think I'll retire."

"So soon?" Ruth asked.

"It has been a long day and I'm really tired."

"See you bright and early tomorrow then," Ruth said.

Kay nodded. "Good evening, Doctor. Thanks for the drink."

He said not a word in reply. His steady gaze never wavered from her face. When she rose to go, his eyes unabashedly ran over her figure.

* * * *

She was relieved she could flee to the quiet of her room. Overbearing, imperious men like Dr. MacDonald, she despised. Didn't she have her fill of men like that? She reflected bitterly over the two years she spent with Biff, a man who used her for his own ends.

Kay went over to the window and opened the louvered shutters. Around the corner of the hotel, Kay saw Ruth and Dr. MacDonald walking hand in hand. Kay stepped quickly away from the window, but not quickly enough because the movement at the window caused the doctor to look up and see her. The ghost of a smile flitted across his face.

Well, she didn't care, although she felt kind of silly peering at people from her window. She explored the drawer in the teakwood desk and found a few sheets of stationery. It seemed as good a time as any to sit down to write to a couple of the girls she had become acquainted with in her opticianry class and to whom she had promised to remain in touch. They had left Hilldale before her and would be surprised to learn where she was.

When she had finished she knew there was one more letter she should write, although she was looking for excuses to postpone it, and that was to Uncle Ted. Uncle Ted never was one to correspond, but she supposed that she did owe him something, at least the courtesy of informing him she had arrived safely.

Hurriedly, she penned a few lines on a half sheet of paper, slipped it into an envelope, sealed it, and placed it with the other two letters when she heard Ruth's voice in the hall say, "Goodnight, Mac." Kay heard Ruth's footsteps pass by her room, then recede. The unmistakable opening and closing of a door followed and then all was quiet.

Kay waited a few minutes. Confident she wouldn't be meeting either Ruth or Dr. MacDonald, she took the three letters she had written and went downstairs in the lobby to deposit them in the mail drop.

She was about to return to her room when, on a sudden impulse, she decided to explore the hotel garden she had glimpsed on first arriving. Although it was already 10:00 o'clock, Kay felt little fear about being out there alone. The garden was well illuminated. The narrow stone path that ran through it was easy to see.

There was a gazebo in the middle of the yard. She followed the path as it looped around the entire length of the garden, past the gazebo. She stopped abruptly, startled to see the silhouette of a man standing in the gazebo, a pipe clenched between his teeth. The silhouette came to life as he took the pipe out of his mouth.

"Good evening, Miss Thompson. Isn't it past your bedtime?"

"Oh. Hello, Doctor. I thought you were in the hotel."

"Is that why you came out here, because you knew you could avoid me?"

"No, of course not. I saw the garden when I arrived and it intrigued me."

"Rather a strange time to admire flowers, wouldn't you say?"

"If you're a flower lover," Kay replied, "any time is a good time to see flowers."

"I don't claim to be an expert. But I think flowers should be viewed in the daytime." With that, he left the gazebo and joined her on the path. He paused to relight his pipe. "Besides, I thought you said you were going to retire early."

"I had all good intentions to do so, but then came downstairs to post a few letters and decided on the spur of the moment to stroll in the garden."

"Spoken like a true creature of impulse." He puffed on his pipe as he walked away from her, discreetly keeping his distance so as not to come too near her.

"I hope this isn't an example of the kind of performance you're going to give us at the clinic, Miss Thompson."

"Why should it be?" Kay asked, her tone of voice conveying the irritation she felt towards him.

"Impulsive behavior doesn't belong in a health care situation," he said evenly.

"Who said it did?"

"Sometimes inexperienced people listen to their hearts instead of their heads."

"If you're implying that I won't or can't follow orders, you're wrong."

"I'm not implying anything," he said. "As long as you understand the game rules."

"I'm a big girl, Doctor, and know my way around."

"I'm sure you do."

"You'll also find, Doctor, that I don't intimidate easily."

"More's the pity," he said, throwing his head back and laughing heartily.

"I know I have a lot to learn," Kay said. "However, I hope to give my best shot for whatever is needed."

"I'm sure you will. Now if you will excuse me, Miss Thompson, good night and I'll see you in the morning."

What was there about this man that persisted to rankle her, even when he tried to soften his remarks. She was bound and determined to put forth her best efforts because a recommendation from Dr. MacDonald would go far in her securing a good position when she returned home.

She climbed the circular staircase to her room. The

hall above seemed empty. She never noticed that it was more dimly lit than before. A single wall bracket near her room threw a deep shadow on the recessed door.

There was someone standing at her door. Kay blinked, uncomprehending. No mistake about it. The outline of a man was there. She gripped the bannister and felt a chill travel the length of her body. She remained frozen on the stairs, unable to speak or call out to the intruder, whoever he was. She squinted.

Was that Dr. MacDonald? Why would he be at her door? Why would he bother to come to her room? She didn't know who it was and was afraid to find out.

Trembling, she retreated down the steps and headed for the lobby. The night clerk smiled when he saw her.

"*Mademoiselle*, what can I do for you?"

"There's a man standing by my door. I've never seen him before."

"Want me to escort you to your room?"

"Please," she said.

He strode briskly to her side "You're not expecting anyone?" the clerk asked.

"No one."

They climbed the steps together. There was no one at the door. Of course, he had had ample time to leave unobserved.

"We could use more light up here," the clerk said. "There's another wall sconce that burned out. Maybe you mistook the shadow." He smiled indulgently at her, and patted her arm as if she were a child afraid of the dark.

"May I have your key? Wait here. I'll go in to check someone isn't hiding in a closet or the bathroom."

Kay shuddered at the thought. She watched him turn the knob before fitting the key in the lock.

"Your door's open, *Mademoiselle*."

Now she remembered. She had left her room hurriedly with only the idea of posting her letters, but then, once downstairs, decided to walk in the garden.

A few seconds later, the desk clerk emerged in the hall. "Everything is fine, mademoiselle. *Bonne nuit.*" He gave her a mock salute and left.

Despite the all clear sign, she felt jumpy. Nothing seemed out of place. Maybe she had imagined that shadow of a man at the door.

She wanted desperately to believe that coming to Haiti was a wise decision, a chance to flee and leave behind anything remotely reminding her of Biff. She wanted to put all those memories behind her.

Tears filled her eyes as she recalled only too vividly how he used her. And she had thought working with him was going to be the springboard she needed to push her into the big time.

Four years ago when she answered that ad in the local paper for a photographer's model, she thought at last she could break out of her humdrum existence.

There was no doubt Biff was good. At first she modeled for a local dress shop for the *DAILY EXPRESS*. A new optical salon opened its doors and she and Biff were suddenly doing sunglass ads, ads that were published in an optical trade publication.

From then on, they were getting calls from around the country, and especially, Chicago, to do more sunglass ads. Biff moved into a bigger studio. Their climb upward was meteoric. But Biff seemed to think that their success together gave him the license to control her life. Biff was too sophisticated for her at that time and she too trusting . . . until he pushed her a little too far.

She smiled, recalling how she got back at him by walking out on him in the middle of a shoot.

"Without me, you're nothing," he had yelled.

"And without me, what have you got? You think that anyone else is going to put up with what I've had to put up with these past years?"

"You can always be replaced," he said coolly.

"Fine. Glad to know I won't be missed."

She walked off the set.

"Hey, you can't do that."

"Oh, can't I?"

"How am I going to pay the rent for this place?"

"That's your problem, not mine."

"I'll sue you for breach of contract."

"So sue me, who cares?" Kay had slammed the door behind her.

It was hard for her now to believe the past had not been a lie. What else to call it? She didn't want to feel used, but wasn't that what Biff was doing? The last she heard about him was that he had moved to Chicago. His name had been linked to some kind of scam that was bilking senior citizens, but nothing had ever been proved. It took her a long time to realize he was a little short in the ethics department. Well, the farther away the better, as far as she was concerned. Thank goodness, she got another chance to change her life by enrolling in the opticianry course.

Time to forget all that. Tomorrow morning would be her first day in a new career at the clinic and she was excited about the prospect of helping the patients. She was going to enjoy every minute of it. In some respects, she dreaded the demands she knew Dr. MacDonald was going to impose on her.

She made a moue. She had almost forgotten the "other demand."

That last day of class, the dean had called her into his office. She thought he was going to wish her a *bon voyage*. Instead, he introduced her to Tom Willoughby from U.S. Customs.

Mr. Willoughby explained that thousands of pairs of counterfeit sunglasses were entering the U.S., along with other fake designer frames.

Kay's mind leaped ahead. "But what has that got to do with me?" she asked, almost fearfully.

"For one thing, aside from your new opticianry training, your experience modeling sunglasses is a plus because you most likely are familiar with the popular styles and designer models on the market.

"At Customs, we think that the counterfeit sunglasses, for instance, are coming through Haiti. Countries where counterfeit goods typically originate are Taiwan, South Korea, Italy, and Brazil. Because the route to the U.S. from Brazil is being watched, the shipments have stopped and we believe that the shipments from Brazil might now be entering the U.S. via Haiti. We need your help, Kay."

"I don't think I'd be any good to you. I don't have any experience in this sort of thing."

"All the better. Your inexperience makes you a natural for us. No one would suspect you of your involvement."

"The truth is I'm not even sure I want to get involved in something like this."

"There will really be no danger to you, personally."

"If this would mean spying on all the people I'm working with, I don't like that idea at all. Besides, they would soon figure out something strange was going on and no one would trust me."

"Kay, you're only going to be in Haiti a short time and when you have to leave, everything will be long gone and forgotten. There'd be no reason for your cover to be blown."

"Well, I don't know. I mean, I'd have to give it some thought." Kay hesitated. "Will I have to carry a gun?"

"No, no nothing like that. Kay, you don't have to worry about violence. All we want you to do is to report anything suspicious."

"Like what?"

"Suppose you were to find some boxes of sunglasses hidden and you suspect they might be counterfeit, we'd like you to tell our agent."

"Who's that?"

"I can't tell you yet, but he will contact you once I give him the word you're part of the team. As soon as he knows and finds you, he will use the code word TRIPWIRE when he meets you. In the meantime, I expect you to keep this information confidential. Anyone you meet at the clinic will be suspect."

She remembered she felt a little ill at ease after that, but then caught up with the excitement of going to Haiti and packing for her trip, she quickly forgot what she might be inviting.

Time to relax. She might not see anything or hear anything during her entire stay here, so why worry?

She got ready for bed, pulled the bedspread off, and there, pinned to the pillow was a note waiting for her: "I've got your number."

She shrank away from the bed. So she did see someone at her door and whoever it was had entered her room and wanted her to know he had been there. She shuddered, sick at heart. Who could or would even dare to do this? Touch her pillow.

Desperately, she racked her brain for a clue. No one knew she was in Haiti except her uncle. She was afraid now to admit the obvious: Someone knew of her undercover assignment for Customs. She wished she had never gotten involved.

She felt unsafe, threatened, fearful for her life. All she wanted to do was to come to Haiti to help in the clinic.

What was worse, she didn't know who to turn to. Certainly, not the police. She wasn't supposed to reveal her mission to anyone except to Tripwire.

She walked over to the window and checked the latch, assuring herself it was locked. There was a double lock on the door. Her hands were shaking when she placed the only chair in the room under the doorknob. If anyone tried to break in while she slept, she'd awake, and be able to scream for help.

Despite the fact she had locked herself in her room, she was on edge. She removed the note from the pillow, turned the pillow over, and crawled into bed. Although she had trouble falling asleep right away, fear, fatigue, and jet lag soon took their toll.

Then she began to dream. She found herself in a place she didn't recognize, surrounded by jungle and enormous plants that dwarfed her. She seemed lost and didn't know where to turn. There was someone standing nearby in shadow. She couldn't see his face, but he looked vaguely familiar. He had been running and so had she. She was quite out of breath.

The man emerged from the shadows. It was Dr. MacDonald. His lips were moving. He was speaking to her, but she couldn't understand him. It didn't seem real. Then he lunged, without warning, in her direction and she, frightened, panicked, started to run.

She awakened with a start, her heart pounding, fearing for her own safety. She didn't know why she had awakened so quickly. Was there a noise in the hall? She slipped out of bed and walked over to the door, placing her ear on it and listened. There was nothing out there, she was positive. The door was still locked and the chair she had placed under the knob was undisturbed.

Noiselessly, she glided over to the window and opened the shutters. It was still dark outside except where the moon cast its silvery spell. Relieved, she returned to bed.

Chapter 2

Kay awoke with a start.

She wasn't dreaming. That was a thump at the door. Another broadside thwacked. The door shuddered, dislodging the chair from its position under the knob and sending it skittering across the floor.

Kay slipped out of bed and tiptoed over to the door. Her heart pounded so loudly she was sure the intruders could hear her.

"What was that?" rasped a male voice she did not recognize.

"Something fell."

"Take it easy, buddy, you'll wake everybody."

Kay grabbed the chair and braced herself for the attack. Could she scream loud enough for help when the door caved in? Her hands were icy and she shivered in spite of herself. To think that all her experience in Haiti boiled down to something like this.

"Is Yvonne in there?" asked the first voice.

"No, she's gone to the States for nurse's training."

"Oh yeah, so who's in there now?"

"I don't know. Maybe no one. Try the door again."

Kay recoiled. She watched the doorknob rotate as it clicked back and forth.

"This is getting us nowheres. Let's get the key from the front desk."

Kay collapsed on the bed, all but drained, her hands still trembling. This couldn't be happening to her. She came all the way from Iowa to help poor people. She couldn't think, as if her mind and heart had stopped. She roused herself suddenly to dress for the clinic.

At least they weren't the ones who pinned the note to her pillow. The note, obviously, was not for Yvonne, since they know she's gone. Whoever wrote that note is aware of Tripwire.

But who are these men who tried to break into her room? What's in this room that they want? What if they rammed their way in while she slept? The thought alarmed her.

She changed quickly into one of the buff colored uniforms she had brought with her. A pair of matching moccasins with wedge heels completed her dress.

Before entering the dining room, she stopped at the front desk. "Would anyone have access to keys to my room?" she asked the clerk.

"Only our maintenance men can get the keys from the desk, and then only when we assign the work in a room."

She still pondered over this when she went to the lobby to meet Dr. MacDonald. Her concerns were interrupted by Ruth.

"Kay, Doctor had to leave early this morning to take care of an emergency case, so I'll run you over to the clinic."

In the jeep, all Ruth could talk about was the emergency case, as if it were a medical breakthrough. Kay wondered if it were concern that motivated such disclosure or a desire to show off familiarity with the doctor.

"A five year old girl was hit in the eye with a stick or a

stone, nobody seems to know, thrown by another five year old."

"Is she badly hurt?" Kay asked.

"I suppose Mac won't know until he's through with his examination. Most likely, Doctor will keep little Nicole at the clinic for a few nights to observe her. If anyone can help her, it will be Mac."

They drove in silence for a few minutes. "Kay," Ruth said, "I don't know how to begin but don't be upset because Dr. Mac thought you were younger than your age. In a way, it's complimentary. Since he's thirty-seven, he thinks anyone under thirty is a . . ."

"Kid?" Kay interrupted.

"No, I wasn't going to say that. I mean . . . well . . . quite young. If it soothes your injured ego any, I think his remarks to you bothered him. When I left him last night in the lobby, he was smoking his pipe and said he was going back into the garden for a few minutes. But he was brooding about something."

"It's not necessary to apologize for the doctor. I don't mean to be rude, but really, you don't have to console me." Eager to steer the conversation into another channel, Kay continued, "Tell me, how long have you been at the clinic?"

"Five months, but Mac has been here for eight."

"Do you volunteer every year for the service?"

"Not exactly. This is a first experience for both of us. Mac is from Boston and that's where we met. I had just been divorced and I guess you can say that we became acquainted at a time when I really needed someone. I tried to tie the loose ends of my life together and Mac suggested I spend a month or two in Haiti because I'd easily forget about my own personal problems, and I have. Helping people in worse circumstances than one's own is always therapeutic. You can see what happened to me. The two months became five and I still hate the idea of leaving. These people are an answer to a volunteer's prayer—happy, cooperative, and so appreciative of anything done for them."

"Is that where Dr. MacDonald practices medicine, in Boston?" Kay asked.

"He's in partnership with another ophthalmologist and when Mac returns, his partner will come down for a month or two."

"How does Dr. MacDonald's family feel about these long absences?"

"Mac isn't married. Medicine is a jealous mistress, it's said. Maybe that's why I understand him and what he needs in his life. Being with Mac, anyway, has been an experience in itself."

"I'm sure it has," Kay said dryly.

"Are you settled in now?" Ruth asked.

"Yes, I am, which reminds me. Do you know who stayed in my room last?"

"I'd have to stop and think about that for awhile. Are you getting her mail or what?"

"Not exactly. There were some people at the door, inquiring about her."

Ruth snapped her fingers suddenly. "Now I remember the girl who had your room. She was a Haitian, name's Yvonne."

"Where is she now?"

"She went to the States for nurse's training. She had been here the first month Mac was here. There was some kind of a problem that developed, I don't recall." Ruth frowned. "Wait." She placed her hand on Kay's shoulder. "I know. She used to play cards with a couple of the maintenance men from the hotel on their lunch hour. She actually left the clinic to meet them."

"Where?" asked Kay.

"In the room you're in now, I believe."

A sense of relief washed over Kay. Maybe that's what that early morning attempted entry was all about. But that wasn't the lunch hour, Kay mused.

"Anyway," Ruth continued, "Mac pressured Yvonne to leave. But if someone is inquiring about her, you should alert

Mac because he indicated that whatever happened, he does not want that girl back under any circumstances.

"Oh, Kay, before I forget," Ruth said, pulling into her parking slot, "the hotel sends over sandwiches for everyone at noon so we don't have to run back and forth eating and losing time here at the clinic. I'll take you to your location and show you where things are."

Kay followed her obediently. Haitians were already queued up in the hall waiting for attention.

"Good morning, Ruth," said Jim Barlow, as they passed by, "and Kay," giving her a wink. Both women waved to him.

Ruth nodded a greeting to the two optometrists, already busy at work, and led the way over to Kay's assigned area.

"Here are all the glasses you'll be using," she said, pointing to two large boxes filled to overflowing.

"These aren't exactly designer frames," Ruth said, as Kay scooped up a Harlequin style in tortoise shell. "That one, for instance, went out of fashion a few years ago."

"Yes, I know," Kay said. "Then came the granny glasses and now the biggies are going strong. No Ray-Bans in this collection?"

Ruth was silent for a moment and when she didn't reply at first, Kay looked up into a face that was far from friendly.

"Ray-Bans would be a luxury item in this part of the world," Ruth said slowly, "especially, since we depend on contributions from schools and service clubs like the Lions."

Kay didn't know if this was a confession of innocence, but the hostility bothered her.

Kay continued to poke into the supply of glasses. How was she expected to find any of the fake glasses if she didn't have a single lead? She didn't know where to begin her investigation and whom she should suspect. Ruth, friendly at first, but now hostile when questioned. Dr. Mac, disagreeable and antagonistic. A pattern?

A deliberate attempt to turn her away from a trail that

might prove embarrassing to them? But they don't know she's looking for any contraband. Still, they could be suspicious of anyone.

"Are you looking for anything in particular?" Ruth asked.

"N-no." Kay hadn't realized Ruth was watching her.

"Do you do anything with sunglasses at all?" Kay asked.

Ruth looked at her sharply. "We don't get any contributions. The people we're treating are more interested in just being able to see better through clear lenses. Do you know where we could get our hands on a good supply of sunglasses?"

Was it the way the question was asked or was it the expression in Ruth's eyes? Something here was coming apart.

"What kind of sunglasses could you get us," Ruth pursued, then paused, lowering her voice, "cheaply?"

Kay laughed nervously. "I don't know what you're talking about." Ruth made her feel guilty, of what she didn't know. "I don't have any source of supply."

"If you don't have a source, do you have any kind of a contact we could use from time to time?"

Ignoring the question, Kay reached for a pair of glasses, focusing on the enormous lenses in an oversized frame. "Where do you send your lab work?" she asked.

"There isn't any laboratory. I should say, you're looking at it," Ruth said, gesturing at the boxes of glasses. "All we can do is find a pair of glasses that comes as close as possible to the prescription that the doctor has written and then adjust them to the patient's face. You never answered my question," Ruth persisted, "about a contact."

"I don't know what you're talking about," Kay said, annoyed.

Dr. MacDonald entered the station. "Good morning," he said perfunctorily.

"How did it go, Doctor?" Ruth asked.

"I don't know yet. There's a lot of blood in the eye that

will have to clear. I sewed up the lid laceration and we'll have to keep Nicole quiet for about five days."

"That's going to be the toughest assignment of all," Ruth said. "Kay, this would be a good opportunity to show you our small hospital ward, if you want to call it that, and then you can meet the rest of the Haitian nursing staff."

The three beds designated as the ward were in the rear of the building, separated from the rest of the clinic by a door.

"Does the doctor do his surgery here?" Kay asked.

"Not exactly. Patients go to the hospital in Port-au-Prince."

In one of the beds was little Nicole. A bandage covered the injured eye. From the other eye flowed a never ending stream of tears, accompanied by sobs and sniffles.

The loneliness of the child was pervasive. Kay's heart went out to her. She remembered her own first experience in a hospital. She had had her tonsils removed. It was a month after her parents had been killed in an auto accident and her uncle appeared so cold and inept when it came to comforting her, at a time when terror was compounded on terror. Kay turned her attention to the small patient before her.

"Does she have to have her arms strapped like that?" Kay asked.

"I know it may seem cruel," Ruth explained, "but if she's not in restraints, she'll keep touching that eye."

"No wonder she's so miserable. Is she in pain?"

Ruth shrugged her shoulders. "Maybe. I really don't know."

"Isn't there something you can give her—a shot—a pill?" Then without waiting for a reply, Kay walked over to the night stand. "There's nothing here. Doesn't the doctor keep any drugs around?"

"No," Ruth said, in a low voice.

"I thought they would be available."

"Nobody can dispense them except Mac and he keeps them under lock and key." Ruth looked at her sharply.

"Maybe this will give some relief." Instinctively, Kay knelt down at Nicole's bedside and gently dabbed the child's cheek dry with a tissue. Then she began stroking her forehead and talking to her in soft, soothing tones. The child stopped whimpering and stared at Kay.

"*Bonjour*, Nicole. *Je m'appelle* Kay."

The child looked from Kay to Ruth, bewildered.

"*Je m'appelle*, Kay," Kay repeated.

"I don't think she understands a word of French," Ruth said.

Kay pointed to herself and said, "Kay." Then she pointed at the child and said, "Nicole." The child regarded her silently. Not one to give up, Kay tried again, first pointing to herself and saying, "Kay." She was ready to point at the child again when Nicole said, "K-Kay." Kay smiled at her and repeated, pointing to herself, "Kay."

"Kay-Kay," the child said again, with greater assurance.

"At least you've accomplished something this morning," Ruth said.

"Isn't Nicole's mother around," Kay asked, "or anyone the youngster knows?"

"No, I'm afraid not," Ruth said.

"The poor thing is crying herself hoarse."

"There's not much we can do about it, We don't have the time or manpower to sit here and hold hands with our pediatric patients."

"How about getting the show on the road, ladies?" The brusque tone of voice was none too familiar.

"I'll leave you for now, Kay," Ruth said.

"Miss Thompson, my remarks are directed to you."

Kay rose slowly from Nicole's bedside. She met the doctor's gaze straightaway.

"In any case, you're dressed for the occasion," he said, his eyes flicking quickly over her. "There's no necessity to play Florence Nightingale. We have work to do." He gestured for her to precede him. "By the way, do you speak French?"

"Yes, a little."

"Not too many people in the hinterland of Haiti know French, but there's always the chance you might run across a few."

"I thought everybody in Haiti spoke French," Kay said.

"Most of our patients speak a kind of Creole patois, which is a mixture of French, Spanish, Indian, African, and even English. There is an elite ruling group, mulatto, in Port-au-Prince, very well educated, who do speak French, but you won't find any of them coming out here for medical care."

While he spoke, he took her arm and pushed her along the corridor. She was glad when they reached her desk.

"Here's what I want you to do," he said. "Get the patient's name, age, vocation, and visual complaint. Now, if he has been here before, most likely, you'll find his chart in the files behind you. Record all your new information on these 5 x 8 cards. Got it?"

Kay nodded.

"If the patient needs glasses, I'll send him back to you with his prescription after my examination. Any questions?"

"None I can think of at the moment."

"Then I'll introduce you to your interpreter."

His name was Jean-Pierre, a tall, lean muscled Haitian whose skin was an exquisite *cafe-au-lait*. No welcome could have been more expansive than the broad grin he flashed her.

"*Parlez-vous francais, Mademoiselle?*"

"*Un peu,*" Kay said.

"All right, you two, stop wasting time and get that line moving," Dr. MacDonald said.

Jean-Pierre shrugged his shoulders in response. Kay took her seat behind the counter that served as a desk and oriented herself. Behind her were a couple of filing cabinets which contained the old patient charts. On the floor to her right were the boxes of eyeglasses she was to use. She nodded to Jean-Pierre she was ready to begin.

The first patient to step forward was a thirty-two-year-old man who sold flowers on the streets of Port-au-Prince. He complained he couldn't see too clearly in the distance. Kay wrote out everything on the file card and escorted the patient over to Dr. MacDonald's cubicle.

She returned to Jean-Pierre who beckoned to the next patient. In rapid succession, Jean-Pierre interviewed three more patients. The four patients returned to the waiting room where they would remain until called by Dr. MacDonald.

Shortly afterwards, the doctor led the first patient back to Kay and gave her the required prescription for glasses.

When the second patient emerged from Dr. MacDonald's examining room, Kay was still busy adjusting the first patient's glasses.

"Jean-Pierre, tell this man please, to sit in the waiting room until I call him."

"Say, what's the bottleneck down there?" Dr. MacDonald shouted.

She refused to recognize either the questioner or his question. At the moment she was struggling with the difficulties of keeping the patient's glasses from sliding down his nose. Baffled, Kay had done everything she could think of, short of performing plastic surgery.

"Miss Thompson, I'm speaking to you." Dr. MacDonald hovered dangerously near. "I thought you didn't have any questions," he said, enjoying her frustration.

"Well, I do now," Kay snapped.

"The only way to keep that pair of glasses from sliding is to use a couple of nose pads." He extracted two from the cabinet behind her.

"Do you know how to affix these?" he asked.

"Yes."

"You're sure? For heavens' sakes, Miss Thompson, stop looking so offended. This is not a classroom. These people need help and are looking to us for help and what we don't need now are," he paused for effect, "amateurs."

"I can adjust the nose pads, Doctor. Thank you."

He stayed to watch. Kay's fingers seemed to be all thumbs as she tried to put the pads in place. She was angry with herself for not being able to make her fingers perform the way she wanted them to and she was angry with Dr. MacDonald for watching her. Her hands were actually shaking.

It was stupid. Come hell or high water, she had no intentions of surrendering the glasses.

"I'll show you an easy way to do this," he said.

"I've almost got them," she said.

"Give the glasses to me," MacDonald ordered.

She ignored him. "Time is awasting, Miss Thompson, and you're holding up the works here. Now give them to me." That's all I need in this operation—another stubborn female, Mac thought.

"There!" Kay said at last, exulting. She wanted to whoop, "I did it after all."

"What do you want me to do, Miss Thompson, give you a gold star for effort?" With that, he beckoned to his next patient and disappeared into the examining room.

The rest of the morning went smoothly enough. Once Kay had run through the routine a couple of times, it became second nature to her and she felt secure in her duties.

After his initial outburst, Dr. MacDonald had little to say to her as he accepted the patient cards she handed him and acknowledged the patients.

At lunchtime Jean-Pierre led the way in the backyard and selected a table for them. "You didn't get yourself anything to drink," he observed. "There's some bottled water in the fridge. I'll bring you some."

When he left, Dr. MacDonald wandered out towards the tables and slid in next to Kay.

Kay turned a triumphant gaze on him. "I'm sorry, Doctor, but Jean-Pierre was sitting there."

"I deserved that," he said, in his best conciliatory manner. "If I promise to behave, do you think I could reserve a seat next to you for tomorrow?"

Kay giggled in spite of herself as she watched him move away to another table.

Jean-Pierre returned with a quart of bottled spring water and poured out a paper cupful. "We eat in shifts," he explained, "because we can't very well close the place down at lunchtime."

"It's a good thing you came to Haiti when you did, he said, "right after our rainy season when I think Haiti is at her most beautiful. Are you planning to do any sightseeing while you're here?"

"Depends on how much free time I have."

"Everyone gets at least one day off a week."

"Good, then most likely I will."

"There are some things you should definitely see before leaving Haiti and one is the Iron Market in Port-au-Prince."

"That's the Moroccan bazaar, isn't it?" Kay asked.

"Bazaar, yes; but Moroccan, no. Talk to me if you decide to go. I'll give you some tips on how to get there and what to buy."

When Jean-Pierre left, Kay was joined by Jim Barlow. It wasn't hard to like him. His red hair was an invitation to friendliness. He settled his tall, gangling form next to her.

"Well, how's it going?" he asked.

"So far, so good."

"Don't let Mac spook you," he whispered to her. "He's a stickler for detail and tends to forget when a volunteer is here for the first time that the routine is new to him or her."

"Thanks for the morale booster," Kay said, casting a quick look in Mac's direction.

"Whatever happens," Jim said softly, "don't let him get you down."

"So tell me, when are you and Mary Ellen getting married?"

"Soon as I finish my education. I have a year and half to go. I bet you'll be invited to our wedding."

Kay smiled. "I already am. Mary Ellen promised me I'd be a bridesmaid."

"Listen, Kay, I've got only a couple of weeks left before I return to the States but I could squire you around and show you the sights or whatever you wanted to do." He rose to go. "Think it over," he yelled back to her as he dashed back to the clinic.

Before Kay returned to her work station, she took a detour to the rear of the building to see Nicole. The child was sound asleep. The tear stains had left streaks on the smooth nut-brown cheeks. An arc of tightly kinked curls on top of her head gave Nicole such a cherubic innocence, Kay wanted to cradle her.

The afternoon whizzed by. Kay saw so many patients that at times she felt that if she hadn't actually seen them standing in line, she would have sworn they were being catapulted towards her from some unknown point in space.

As the afternoon drew to a close, Kay looked forward to the promise of a warm shower and a quiet dinner. She stooped down to retrieve some glasses when she heard Ruth's voice.

"How's the glamourpuss doing?"

"Hard to say," was Mac's reply.

"Something wrong?"

"I wonder if this is a sting operation."

"Mac, what are you talking about?"

"Ever since that damned malpractice suit, I've been uneasy about a lot of things."

"Whatever are you worried about? You were cleared on that over a year ago."

"I can't afford to get myself ensnared in any government-sponsored scam. That malpractice suit was bad enough."

"Mac, you weren't even guilty. How could you possibly know those intraocular lenses were contraband."

"Yeah, well."

"Are you suspicious of Kay?"

"In a way."

"You're getting paranoid."

"For someone who was allegedly trained as an optician, she struggled putting on some nose pads on a pair of glasses. Would you believe it?"

Ruth laughed. "That's no evidence of anything. Could be a case of first day jitters."

"Is it? Every inexperienced optician I've encountered knows how to put on nose pads. You don't need any technical training for that."

"She came with a recommendation from the opticianry school."

"That could be faked. Do you think she could be an investigative reporter?"

"I don't know, but maybe," Ruth said slowly and deliberately. "I never thought of that."

"Which means what?"

"Kay had asked some strange questions."

'Such as?"

'For one thing, she noticed we didn't have any Ray-Ban sunglasses on hand."

"Did she actually mention Ray-Ban by name?"

"Oh yes, and she also seemed concerned about the accessibility of drugs."

"What did you tell her?"

"You were the only one who dispensed them."

Kay restrained herself from jumping up and speaking in her defense. She didn't say drugs, meaning narcotics. She meant drugs as medications. This is absolutely stupid. They think she's a suspect in something illegal. Why was Ruth twisting her words?

"I better get going, Mac," Ruth said.

"One word before you go. Keep an eye on her."

"I sure will, as long as you don't. See you tomorrow."

Kay scurried down the hall so as not to be seen. It was

Ruth who hailed her. "Dr. Mac will give you a lift back to the hotel. I've got to run."

And where can you possibly run in a place like Haiti, thought Kay.

Dr. MacDonald emerged from his cubicle. "Come on, Kay," he said in a proprietary fashion, "we've got lots of things to discuss." He propelled her to the jeep.

"Well, tell me, how did your first day go?" he asked, as they settled down for the drive back to the hotel.

You ought to know. You were there, she wanted to say. Instead, she said, "Fairly well."

"Any questions?"

"No," she said, too weary to pursue it any further.

"If you want to ask about any of the procedures today, I promise I won't bite. Ruth tells me that someone at your door was inquiring about Yvonne."

Kay was surprised that he brought it up. Maybe this was more serious than she thought.

"I wouldn't worry too much about it. Yvonne was the girl who had occupied your room before you and unfortunately, she got herself into a lot of problems."

"Like drugs?"

He looked at her sharply. "No, it wasn't drugs this time, but other entanglements. Nothing for you to worry your pretty head about. That girl has a chance to do something worthwhile in her life now and I hope she does. Are you sure that you don't want to ask anything about the routine today?"

Kay smiled at his attempt to be sociable. "I really don't have any questions right now."

"Good. Then I have a few questions for you. I couldn't help but overhear Jim's remarks to you at lunch about urging you to think it over before he left. Is he zeroing in on you?"

His inference irritated her. "I don't think that's any of your business, Doctor."

"On the contrary, it is. I'm in charge of the volunteers

here and I'm interested in seeing them work efficiently and they can't if there are any problems, personal or otherwise, interfering with their efficiency."

"Tell me the truth, Kay, is Jim giving you the rush act?"

"Doctor, no one gives me the rush act, if I don't want it."

Dr. MacDonald chuckled. "Don't tell me you're giving him the rush act."

"Still think I'm on a fishing expedition, don't you?"

"There are other words for that, but I don't think this is the time and place." He grinned good-naturedly at her.

Kay turned her head away from him and pretended to focus on the scenery they passed. She was glad when they arrived at the hotel. The day had been a full one and despite Dr. MacDonald's attitude towards her, there was a lot of satisfaction in what she was doing. Ruth was right. The work itself was its own reward.

As soon as she entered her room, she scrutinized everything to see if anyone had entered and searched her things. She had left the drawer in the desk ajar deliberately and it was the same. She had also left some coins on the desk. They were still there, untouched.

Downstairs, Mac stopped to speak to Michel. "Did you get that attaché case I left at the desk yesterday?"

"Yes, Doctor, and I got your message about putting it in the closet in your room."

"So where is it? It's not in my room."

"Doctor, I know I put it there because you were kind enough to leave your door open for me."

"Michel, my door was locked. That's why I had asked you to leave it there because I didn't have my room key with me at the time."

"Oh, Doctor, I'm sorry."

"Which room did you put it in?"

"Number Six at the top of the stairs."

"That's all right, Michel. I know you're new," he said, not wishing to offend him, "but that was the wrong room."

"Doctor, I'm so sorry. But can you get it?"

"Don't worry about it, now that I know where the case is." So little innocent has had the attaché case all along and then she left her door open. Why? So her expected visitor can enter easily? Does she still have the stuff in her possession or did she give it away already or sell it to the highest bidder?

. . . .

Kay showered leisurely and reached for her lime sheath from the closet and then she saw the attaché case. It looked like the same one that Dr. MacDonald retrieved at the airport. She frowned. Of course, most attaché cases do look alike. She pulled it out into the room. It wasn't locked, which made her more suspicious than ever. She flipped it open and almost cried out in surprise.

There were Ray-Ban sunglasses along with designer frames, Christian Dior, Ralph Lauren, Bill Blass. There were two of each. A note was tucked in between two pairs of the Ray-Bans, "Doctor, I think you could make good use of these." No signature. If she had any doubts about the case, they were dispelled now.

A feeling of revulsion swept over her. She removed the Ray-Bans. It wasn't difficult to identify the genuine pair. The fake one had Ban spelled with two *N*s, and also had inferior lenses, she knew.

She picked up a couple of the Christian Dior designer frames. She knew immediately which one was the counterfeit. The quality of the hinge on the genuine Dior was a clear signal for those in the know.

She hurriedly put the frames back in the case. Strange, that the case should be unlocked. How could she get in touch with Mr. Willoughby? She couldn't go anywhere. She was virtually isolated. She had no one to contact. She was in a state of limbo and then suddenly, anger followed.

Why, anyway, was she involved in this caper? All she

had wanted in the first place was just to come to Haiti and help people.

On top of everything, she didn't even have a decent place to hide the evidence. So, Mac was up to his neck in some kind of illegal operation. Oh, for a magic lamp to rub to make Tripwire appear. She closed the case and stashed it further back in the closet than before.

She finished dressing and walked downstairs to the dining room. She was waiting to be seated when a hand casually caught her elbow and pushed her gently forward.

"I have a table right this way."

Kay didn't want to make a scene, but as soon as she was seated she didn't mince any words. "Doctor, you may be my boss during working hours, but after hours, my time is my own."

He looked up from the menu, frowned, and said, "I'd recommend the one-pot dish of shrimp, rice, and lima beans. It's a good Haitian dish. With that, we get a green salad with vinaigrette dressing and some marvelous crusty French bread." He gave the order to the waiter and then added, "Oh yes, and some white wine. Let's see—Chassagne-Montrachet 1970."

The waiter acknowledged the order and left. Dr. MacDonald turned all of his attention to Kay. "Now what was this about your life after hours?"

Kay remained silent.

"Truthfully, I didn't think you wanted to eat alone. I sure didn't and since I already was seated at a table, I thought we might as well enjoy each other's company."

There was a faint glimmer of amusement in the slate blue eyes across the table from Kay. She lowered her gaze.

"I think you'll find that the Haitian and French cuisines prepared here are excellent."

The waiter brought their dinners then. The doctor watched Kay chew the first couple of mouthfuls.

"Was that really so awful?" he asked. The twinkle was still in his eyes.

"I never said it was," Kay said. "It's delicious. But I don't appreciate someone coming in and taking charge of my life."

"Is that so?" he asked, the corners of his mouth quirked up in a grin. "And who's the ogre who has been taking charge of your life up to now?"

"No one has . . . or will," she said emphatically, bringing her chin up defiantly.

"What do your parents think about your running off to another country?"

"My parents are dead. I've been living with an uncle."

The doctor's full attention was concentrated on her.

"And he doesn't approve your roaming about like this, does he?"

"He wants me to stay put in town." Kay shook her head, as if pleading her case.

"So he can keep an eye on you?"

"I suppose so."

"Didn't you say you were a model? Your resumé said Chicago."

Kay nodded.

"That should have made your uncle realize you were a big girl now."

"If it only were that simple."

"How did he ever allow you to go to Chicago in the first place?"

"He didn't like the idea at all, but he had no voice in the matter."

"Oh really?"

"I answered an ad for a photographer's model and the photographer and I became quite successful, first doing local newspaper ads and then on to Chicago for national ads."

"What did you model—dresses, sportswear?"

"Sunglasses."

"Any particular brand?"

"Ray-Ban."

"I see." I see a lot of things, he thought. Could she possibly be that naive about the copycat game? This was beginning to smell like a scam. Why would she admit to Ray Ban so easily, unless she has everything neatly sewn up, and she's warning me to stay out of her way. Hard to believe she would be involved in this very dangerous game. Must be those freckles that make her appear so virtuous.

"Whatever made you leave the modeling, or shouldn't I ask?"

You shouldn't ask, Kay thought. "I wasn't getting anything out of the job. I enjoyed it while I was doing it, but I felt it was time to move on to something less frivolous." Even now resentment welled up within her when she thought of those lost years.

Kay shook her head. "I'm sorry. What did you say?"

"I haven't said anything. Whoever he was he doesn't evoke pleasant memories, does he?"

"I really don't care to discuss it. I came to Haiti because I wanted to help and that's all you need to know."

Can I believe her? Has she told me the truth about why she wanted to come or is there a darker secret in her past? Is she really an optician or is she here for another purpose?

"Remember that attaché case I picked up at the airport, Kay?"

Picked up is right, she thought.

"Well, I told the desk clerk to have Michel place it in my room."

What is he getting at, anyway? If he suspects me, why doesn't he come right out and accuse me, instead of playing these silly games.

"Since I never did find it in my room, I wondered if maybe it was placed in your room by mistake."

Isn't that sweet! He knows I've got it. "Why, no, I don't believe I saw it. What would it be doing in my room, if it were supposed to be in your room?"

"You know what it looks like don't you?"

"Oh sure."

Just as she thought. He's up to his neck in a phony frame bit.

"I don't have it," Kay said at last.

"I didn't accuse you of having it. I just wanted to know if you saw it."

Kay turned her attention to the dinner, leaving his comment unanswered.

They finished eating and he ordered brandy for both of them.

"So you think that by working here for a few weeks, you'll be doing something for humanity."

Kay flushed under his scrutiny. "You make me sound sanctimonious."

"You didn't, but I hope you realize that once you've gone, the health needs in this area will continue. Yes, you will have helped, even a little, although your stay is temporary."

"I understand," Kay said.

"I myself will only be here for another couple of weeks or so, then, I, too, have to return to my other obligations. Fortunately, there are volunteers who come frequently enough to take over. Otherwise, I'd feel remiss in my own duties, knowing that these people weren't being cared for."

The ensemble began playing a slow melody.

"Too full of food to dance?" Dr. MacDonald asked.

Kay shook her head. She rose and he slid his arm around her waist, gliding her out to the dance floor. Whether it was his nearness, his woodsy aftershave, or the few sips of brandy she had had, she enjoyed being this close to him.

Perhaps he sensed her sudden vulnerability as he led her out to the terrace.

She saw the expression in his eyes soften as he pulled her to him. The kiss that followed was gentle, gentler than she thought him capable. At first she steeled herself to resist, but couldn't still her own racing pulses. As the pressure on her lips increased, she responded to the overpowering demands of his desire.

Then, without warning, he removed her arms from

around his neck and with a sardonic grin, said, "I thought you didn't come to Haiti for romance."

Kay was humiliated. She stood there, shaking, her legs wobbly, her heart pounding. She hated him. She swung away from him so he couldn't see the tears in her eyes.

Chapter 3

"Dr. Mac, are you out there?" As Ruth Emerson's voice caught them both unawares, Dr. McDonald whirled around and away from Kay.

"We're over here, Ruth," he said.

"Dr. Mac," Ruth said, giving Kay a quick inspection, "Nicole has been kidnapped."

"In my clinic? Impossible. How?"

"No one knows exactly."

"Damn! That eye has got to get rest," Dr. MacDonald said.

"The bandage was pulled off and left in the bed."

He grimaced. "That's the witch doctor's work. Apparently, modern medicine isn't healing that eye fast enough. Did you talk to anyone, Ruth?"

"There wasn't anyone around when I had gone in to check on Nicole."

"I'll go back to the clinic with you." Taking her arm, he left the hotel without a word to Kay.

Kay remained on the terrace and watched the jeep drive away. She was emotionally drained. She was exasperated with herself for succumbing to such passion with only a first kiss. What was the matter with her anyway? Mac, like Biff, another macho type, using women when they were available and dropping them just as readily, whenever it was convenient to do so. Hadn't she learned her lessons from Biff?

There was no doubt what Mac thought about girls who go into modeling. As much as she talked about him, she could not brush off the memory of his kiss. She didn't want to begin to wonder why her thoughts were dominated by it. That, too, was disturbing.

She tried to think of a clue that held the key to his obvious antagonism towards her. Did he suspect that she might interfere with his plans of passing the copycat frames and sunglasses into the USA? She was the one who had the evidence to nail him, and the way she felt now, nothing would make her happier. He probably thought she was going to screw up his plans. Maybe, just maybe.

How else to understand his motives for leading her on the way he did? To lure her into a snare and then manipulate her to his whim, to prove something. What? That she was vulnerable to a male as magnetic as he—or something more dangerous? Smuggling contraband to the U.S. If only she knew who the agent for Tripwire was. Then she'd have at least someone she could talk to that she could trust; someone she could confide in.

She traced the outlines of her lips with her fingertips and smiled in spite of herself. She couldn't deny she'd enjoyed that kiss, trap or no trap. He would soon discover she wouldn't be easily intimidated.

She returned to her room. A note had been slipped under her door. "This is no place for you." A warning or a threat? If only she had been in the room when the messenger delivered this note. At least she'd have had a chance to confront him. She studied the handwriting. Like the other note, this, too, was printed in oversized capital letters.

Kay scrutinized everything to see if anyone had entered and searched her things. She checked the closet. The attaché case with its overwhelming evidence was untouched. Kay frowned. Was Mac behind this? Sure, he suspected she had the attaché case. But he was dining with her and never had the opportunity to get away. He could have given someone else the note to deliver earlier, just before dinner.

She wasn't thinking straight. Even if Mac was behind this, why would he resort to scare tactics when the clinic needs all the help it can get? He didn't know her that well yet and for all he knew she might become so frightened she'd pick up and head for home. Didn't make any sense. Plenty of time to think about it all in the morning.

She rinsed out her uniform and hung it up to dry, then lay thinking about the events of the evening. By all rights, she should be vindictive, but she couldn't.

* * * *

The next morning Dr. MacDonald was waiting for her in the lobby. He greeted her cheerily, as if nothing had happened between them last night.

In the jeep he briefed her about the circumstances leading up to the discovery of the missing Nicole.

"One of the Haitian nurses on duty told me that Nicole's mother had come in and said she wanted to see her daughter. Even though it was after hours, the nurse saw no reason for alarm or to deny the mother access to her own child, who was sleeping at the time. About a half hour later, the nurse went in to check on Nicole and found her gone. The bandage had been ripped off and was left on the pillow."

"Are you going to call the police?" Kay asked.

"The police have enough to do without tailing runaway patients."

"Aren't you going to look for Nicole at all?" Kay asked, surprised at the casual manner in which he related the particulars. The image of a disoriented and frightened child haunted Kay from her own past. She, too, had been awakened abruptly from a deep sleep, when her parents were killed.

"If the mother doesn't return the child, then I'll have to go after her myself, I suppose," he said resignedly, pulling into the clinic parking lot.

Kay reached for the door handle.

"Wait," he said, placing a hand on her arm to detain her. "Kay, about last night—forget it. I want . . ."

"That's exactly what I've already done, Doctor," she interrupted. "Forgotten it."

His eyes raked over her. "As easily as that, eh? I guess I had you figured right all along."

"What did you want me to do? Fall at your feet?"

His eyes clouded at her accusation.

How did he expect her to react to him? His detachment now only served to fire her own emotions. She felt the warmth of her face express the pent-up anger from last night. She wanted to lash out at him with the full strength of her fury and whittle him down to size, after the way he had humiliated her.

"That's a rotten thing to say," he said. The slate blue eyes were opaque.

"Is it?" She left the jeep, slamming the door with the force of her wrath.

"Kay, wait for me," Dr. MacDonald called. How could he respond to her accusation? He never got a chance to say that he was sorry he'd had upset her, but he didn't want her to think he was rushing her. Now she'd never believe him, he was sure.

Kay pretended she hadn't heard him and jogged, then ran towards the entrance to the clinic.

Jean-Pierre was waiting for her when she arrived at her station. She sucked in her breath, attempting to recoup some of the depleted energy she had spent in her show of temper.

• • • •

The morning continued without a hitch. She had little to say to Mac and he barely spoke. It was as if she had made the final pronouncement.

At lunchtime she and Jean-Pierre shared a table. It was the first time Kay had had a chance to get acquainted with him. His knowledge of French, American, and English literature was astounding.

"Whatever are you going to do with all that background?" Kay asked.

"I want to teach, eventually, and hope I can come to the States for graduate work," he said.

"I thought translating was your vocation."

He chuckled. "No, but it might benefit me. Working alongside American doctors and ingratiating myself will enable me to get the recommendation I need for entrance to an American university."

"Jean-Pierre, if there's ever anything I can do in the future, call on me, please, too," Kay said, eager to help.

"Thanks, Kay." He was silent for a moment, as if thinking, then snapped his fingers. "Come to think of it, there is something you could do for me."

Warily, Kay asked, "What?"

"Get the money for me to pay for my education."

Suddenly, Kay felt her reflexes snap to attention. Was he serious? "What exactly did you have in mind?"

"A lot of things, but they're all illegal." He threw his head back and laughed uproariously, then hastily left the table.

She didn't enter the building, but reflected on what he had just said. Was he testing her or was he only kidding?

Returning to her station, Kay waited for Jean-Pierre to join her to start the afternoon schedule when she looked around, wondering why he had left the lunch table so hurriedly. She couldn't see him anywhere. What was the rush? There was only one place to go and that was back inside the clinic.

She watched as two men approached her desk. One was Haitian, the other looked American. Both were dressed in business suits. The Haitian had an ominous habit of keeping one hand in his pocket, as if he had a gun.

"Is the doctor busy?" the American asked. Kay thought his blue eyes were the coldest she had ever seen.

"Could I have your names, please?" Kay asked.

"No," said Blue Eyes. "You tell him we're here and we have got to see him now. He can stop stalling. We can't wait any longer. He knows all about us. Give him this as a calling card." He had written the name of Ray Bann on a small slip of paper.

Kay walked over to Mac's cubicle, knocked on the door, then opened it, since she knew there were no patients there.

"Doctor, there are two men here to see you."

"Who are they?"

"They refused to give me their names."

"Are they patients?"

"I don't think so. They gave me this calling card."

MacDonald studied the name. "Yeah, unfortunately, I know who they are."

"Should I tell them to come here?"

Mac hesitated for a moment, then said, "I'm too busy now to see them."

Kay reported back to the waiting men.

Blue Eyes replied, "You tell him it's damned important for us to see him and if we can't, there will be trouble for him and for all of us." Kay returned to Mac with the message.

"I wish I had never gotten myself involved in the first place," he muttered to himself, as if Kay were not present. Then realizing he had spoken in her presence, his voice became tight as he looked directly at her. "You go out and tell them I don't wish to see them . . . period. They will meet with me at my convenience, and certainly not at the clinic."

She returned to the two waiting men and again gave them Mac's reply.

"You tell the Doc that he's got to get in touch with us in two days or else." With that, they left.

The name of Ray Bann kept resounding in her head. That's the spelling for a copycat Ray-Ban. Mac saw it, knew it. Is it now used as a code word? She didn't have much time for further reflection when Jean-Pierre returned.

"Sorry I'm late, Kay," he said, taking his seat opposite her.

"I was looking for you. Where did you disappear to so fast?"

"Disappeared, right." He laughed. "A minor emergency to attend to, nothing important."

Jean-Pierre called the first patient to begin the afternoon work. Kay wondered what the minor emergency was.

The patients absorbed her and any thoughts she had about Jean-Pierre's suspicious behavior soon evaporated. Now that she was well oriented with the routine, the time sped quickly.

Dr. MacDonald was waiting for her in the jeep at the end of the day. Kay got in beside him, scarcely glancing at him, as he stepped on the accelerator. He turned to her briefly. "Nothing to say after a day's work?"

Kay shook her head. "Those two men who were here want you to call them in a couple of days."

"I have a table reserved for us for dinner," he said, as if he didn't hear her or didn't want to hear her.

Kay said not a word; but when they arrived at the hotel, she bolted for the door and went to her room. She did not want to have dinner with him, but she didn't know how she was going to get out of it. She felt like a child running away from an unpleasant task.

By all rights, she should dine with him to find out if he was involved in Ray-Ban and designer frame copycats. Even if he were, what could she do right now? She couldn't arrest him. She couldn't even call for help from the alleged Tripwire agent. She was beginning to doubt whether the guy even existed. How could she possibly extract any information from Mac? He would know right away the purpose of her questioning and if he knew anything, he certainly wasn't going to admit it to her.

Without catching him red-handed with the evidence, all the questions in the world would be of no value. Suppose she did catch him with the goods, how could she detain him?

The thought of facing Dr. MacDonald at dinner another night, rebuffing his questions and staving off his attentions sobered her. Is that what she wanted? She didn't like what his kiss had done to her.

But how could she dodge him? There was no place for her to go. She couldn't very well get out and start walking somewhere. She was debating as to her course of action when there was a soft knock on the door. The knock was followed by a low voice. "Kay, it's me. Jim Barlow."

Kay opened the door to the optometric student.

"How about dinner and a little night life in Port-au-Prince?"

"Tonight?" Kay asked.

"No better time," he said.

No better time, indeed, she thought. What an ideal way to avoid dining with MacDonald. Jim expected an answer.

"I'll be ready in a few minutes."

"Great! Meet me downstairs," Jim said.

Kay checked out her closet before she showered. The attaché case was still there. She was sure Mac knew where it was. He was probably waiting for her to make the first move.

Dressed in a pale green cotton skirt and blouse with a mandarin collar, she clipped silver petals on her ears, fastened a wide silver bracelet on her arm, and walked downstairs to wait for Jim.

She was standing in the foyer when Dr. MacDonald came up behind her, slipped an arm around her waist, and whispered in her ear, "You're waiting in the wrong place. Our table is over there. I've already ordered a bottle of wine for us."

Another take-charge male. No thank you. She stepped back, freeing herself from his hold, and faced him. "I'm sorry, Doctor, but I have a date tonight."

"With whom?"

"Jim Barlow."

"I thought you and I had a date," he said.

"I never said we had," she said. He raised his hand as if to challenge that statement.

"Yes?" Kay asked.

"Nothing, nothing at all," he said.

There was little satisfaction in rejecting him. The amount of glory she anticipated did not occur. Possibly, she had been too rash in spurning the doctor and accepting Jim's invitation. She was tempted to break her plans with Jim. Before she could change her mind, Jim came bounding down the stairs.

"Oh, Kay, let's go."

As she turned to leave, she saw the doctor, seated in the dining room. He was staring at her and the pang of remorse that filled her was hard to dismiss. Why should she have any regrets anyway? He could always eat with Ruth, Kay thought.

There's no need for him to have that hang dog expression. A wave of resentment swept over her; resentment towards him because he could generate such emotion in her.

"Hey, Kay, are you coming?"

"Right away."

"I decided we better stay in the area," Jim said. "I hope you're not disappointed."

"What happened to your high-flown plans of going to Port-au-Prince?"

"For one thing, it's far and if we stay late, driving that road back is hazardous, unless you want to live dangerously."

"Not particularly. Then where are we going?" Kay asked.

"There's a terrific place down by the beach that specializes in fire-cooked fresh fish and chicken. I think you'll enjoy it. Also, there's good music for dancing."

The food was everything Jim said it was and then some. Kay was relaxed and the vexation she felt towards MacDonald also seemed to disappear. Dancing with Jim was fun only because his line of chatter was so silly.

Unfortunately, his lead was not as strong as the doctor's. More than once, Kay found herself mumbling, "Sorry," as she stumbled over his feet.

"Maybe I ought to give up," he said, leading her back to their table.

They sipped their wine and watched others dance. As Kay turned her attention back to the table, she was disconcerted to find Jim staring at her.

"Jim, what's the matter? Isn't my makeup on straight?"

"You know, Kay," he said dreamily, "you're a great looking girl."

"You're drunk, Jim."

"I'm not drunk. You're gorgeous. I wonder why Mary Ellen never told me anything about you."

"Before or after your engagement?" Kay countered.

"No, really, Kay, you remind me of someone I once knew."

"That's an old line, Jim. Why don't you try something original, like, 'Haven't we met before?'"

"But, Kay, you do remind me of someone . . . someone who stayed in your room last year."

"You mean Yvonne?"

"How did you know?"

"I found out a lot about her. She's in the States now, studying nursing."

"Why were you interested in her?" Jim asked

"Someone had been inquiring about her, so I asked Ruth and she told me. Mac filled in a couple of blanks for me, too."

"I'm sure he did," Jim said. "I'll tell you something they didn't tell you. She was quite a babe. Whew!"

"Well, I didn't expect you to erupt like that."

"Let me give you the facts of life, Kay, my dear. Yvonne could make anything erupt, including Vesuvius."

"Was she involved in something?"

The laughter was gone from his eyes. It was indeed a different Jim that met her gaze. "Whatever you've been told about Yvonne is pure hearsay and rumors, nothing more. All rumors," he repeated. "Was my name linked with hers?"

"No. Should it have been?"

"No. Just checking. Rumors, you know, can ruin a guy's reputation. We probably should be heading back to the hotel."

"So early?" Kay asked. He certainly made short shrift of that conversation.

"It's 11:00 and Dr. MacDonald likes his staff in the hotel by midnight."

"Why? Do our clothes change into rags at the stroke of twelve?"

"I think he feels responsible for us."

"You're kidding! I'm not exactly a sixteen-year-old and neither are you."

"He feels that if we get a good night's rest, we'll be a more efficient staff," he said very seriously.

"Don't tell me he actually called a staff meeting for this."

"Not quite."

"Is that the way he talks to the professionals who leave their practices in the States to come to Haiti and volunteer?"

"His remarks are directed only to the younger members of the group."

"I didn't realize this was a kindergarten operation," Kay said sarcastically.

"It's not, but the clinic had some negative experiences about four months ago with a bevy of cuties, scarcely out of their teens, who spent time partying till the wee hours, then couldn't show up for work the next day because they overslept. If they did report, their productivity left much to be desired."

"Listen, Kay, changing the subject for a minute. Do you happen to have Mary Ellen's new address? I'd like to surprise her by writing first and telling her about meeting you."

"You're in luck because she had rented the new apartment two days before I left home. I'll give you the address when we get back."

Jim and Kay had scarcely entered the hotel when Dr. MacDonald hailed them as they climbed the stairs.

"I've been looking high and low for you, Kay," he called. "I want to talk to you."

"Not now," she said, turning around.

MacDonald ran up the steps. "I've got to talk to you now, Kay."

Her key was in the lock. Swiftly, she turned the knob and entered, ignoring the doctor. She beckoned to Jim to follow and closed the door behind him.

"I wonder what he wanted to talk to you about at this hour," Jim said.

"Couldn't be so important that it can't wait till the morning." Kay dug out Mary Ellen's address from her suitcase and gave it to Jim. "There's hotel stationery in the desk drawer."

Since she had been gone for a few hours, Kay checked out her closet. The attaché case was gone. So that's what he had on his mind.

"Hey, Kay, what's the matter? You look like you just lost your best friend."

The only one who knew she'd be away was Mac. It stood to reason that Mac hadn't had a chance to take the case before since he was at the clinic, and then later he wouldn't dare. But now that he'd so boldly entered her room, she mused, had he written those notes, too? She wouldn't put it past him.

"Come on, sit down over here," Jim said, "and tell me what's happened to you all of a sudden."

"It's really nothing. It was something in my closet and I must have misplaced it."

"Want me to help you look for it?"

"No, no that won't be necessary."

"What is it?"

"Something personal."

He regarded her in amazement, slapping his forehead. "First you lose something that apparently, devastates you. Then you can't tell me what it is. Or is it that you don't want me to know?" He wasn't grinning at her any more, and Kay thought she saw another side of Jim and wondered if Mary Ellen was marrying the right guy after all.

There had been so many times during the evening she'd wanted to confide in Jim, but something held her back. His disarming manner tempted her to believe in him. But now that his behavior, in fits and starts, was strangely suspicious, she was glad she hadn't revealed anything. She couldn't report the theft of the case even if she wanted to.

Silently, she called on her patron saint. *Mr. Willoughby, wherever you are, I need you. Where is the agent, if he exists, that is, who's supposed to whisper sweet nothings in my ear like Tripwire?*

Jim rose to leave. "Think I better go or I won't be able to get up tomorrow."

"Thanks, Jim, for a nice evening."

"Glad you had a good time, even with my dancing. Well, hope you find whatever it is you lost."

* * * *

Next morning Dr. MacDonald was waiting for her in the lobby. She could feel his anger as soon as she saw him. It was the way he stood, legs astride, arms crossed on his chest while he considered her.

He was probably angry because she lied to him about the attaché case. She had no apologies to make. This was not the time to test his amiability as she attempted to walk past him. He did not move, remaining steadfast, and continued to block her path.

Her pulses pounded wildly and she was annoyed that he could effect such a reaction in her, even after their last confrontation.

"Good morning, Doctor," she said blithely, hoping to conceal the huskiness in her voice. "Aren't you driving to the clinic this morning?" Without a word, he headed out towards the jeep.

If he didn't want to talk, that was fine and dandy with her. What did he expect her to do? Hang her head in contrition for an imaginary offense he had contrived? He was probably mad because she ditched him last night, too. Two strikes against her.

"Did you have a good time last night," he asked, as they pulled away from the hotel.

"Very much so," Kay said. "The food was excellent and the music was good, too; perfect for dancing."

"I thought you came in rather late," he stated flatly.

"As long as I'm on the job on time, I don't think that's any concern of yours."

"Whether you like it or not, it does concern me. The school holds me responsible for the welfare of any volunteer it sends. The fact that you were out with Jim . . . "

"What difference would that make?" she interrupted.

Dr. MacDonald was silent for a moment. "A lot of difference," he answered in slow, measured tones. "Everyone at the clinic knows Jim is engaged."

"What's that got to do with me?" Kay asked recklessly, enjoying every minute of his vexation.

He looked at Kay, his eyes narrowing dangerously. "That doesn't mean anything to you?"

"Why should it?"

"You're out to collect as many scalps as you can, aren't you?"

"That's what you've wanted to believe ever since I arrived, isn't it?"

"You can't deny that I saw Jim enter your room and an hour later leave. I'm sure you didn't talk about the price of fish."

"No," Kay said, "that's something I can't deny."

"You're acting like a petulant child declaring your independence."

"And you're acting like a male chauvinist with your demands."

"The only demands I'm making on you have to do with your hours and your punctuality."

"Well, I've been on time, so I don't think you have anything to complain about."

"If I have any complaints, it might be in another department."

She got out of the jeep, puzzled over his response.

He watched her walk to the clinic door. Why didn't he ask her about the attaché case? He'd most likely get the same flip responses he got about her relationship with Jim. Better to tread softly about the case and wait and see.

Jean-Pierre was anxiously pacing the floor inside the entrance. "I was worried you'd be late and we've got a lot of work facing us. One of the nurses was inquiring about a patient card and I told her you'd look for it as soon as you got here."

"Jean-Pierre, you don't have to wait for me for something like that. You can search the files yourself when you need some information."

"I'm only an interpreter."

"No one would bite your head off if you did have to look for something."

They walked down the hall together and Kay scurried around, riffling through the files until she found the specific chart requested and handed it to Jean-Pierre who hurried over to the nurse with it.

The morning sped by with little incident. Either Dr.

MacDonald had given up on her or decided to be on his best behavior because he neither challenged nor offered opposition to anything she did.

At the end of the day, she waited for Jim in the reception room while he finished up.

"Want a ride back to the hotel?" Dr. MacDonald asked, advancing towards her.

"Jim is taking me, thank you."

"You're getting to be quite a twosome these days, aren't you?"

"If you mean because we work in the same place and ride to work together . . ."

"That's not what I mean," he interrupted, "and you know damn well it's not."

He stood very close to her. She could feel his warm breath on her face as he spoke, his eyes never wavering from her. She retreated a little from him and forced herself to look away. She was more than aware of something magnetic, a charge, between them.

"Ready to go, Kay?"

She breathed easier when she heard Jim's voice behind her.

• • •

Back at the hotel, she showered and dressed and was waiting in the lobby for Jim to join her when Dr. MacDonald found her.

"Not dining here tonight?"

Just then Jim took his place next to Kay and slipped an arm around her waist. "Come on, beautiful, let's go."

"Good night, Doctor," Kay said, conscious of the glitter in his eyes, the whiteness of the lines around his mouth as he pressed his lips tightly together, and stared at her, his gaze wandering to Jim's arm around her.

"Hope you don't mind going to the same place for dinner where we were last night," Jim said as they got into his car.

"Not at all," Kay said.

Jim glanced at her briefly. "You know, Kay, you seem to be more relaxed tonight than you were last night."

"Maybe it's because I know your intentions are honorable."

He laughed. "You don't know me very well."

"But I know Mary Ellen," Kay said, "and that says it all."

The evening was enjoyable as before. As for the dancing, Kay realized that Jim's hadn't improved noticeably even after one night.

"Say, did you ever find what you lost," Jim asked nonchalantly.

"No," she said.

He leaned over the table to her. "Anything I can do to help?"

"Really, Jim, it's not that important."

Well, you can't have everything, she thought. At least with Jim she felt safe, safe from the whirl that sent her emotions into a tailspin. That's what was important, wasn't it?

"Tell me about some of the staff—where they're from and how long they've been here." Then before Jim could answer, Kay asked, "Is it true that Dr. MacDonald was named in a malpractice suit?"

"Where did you hear that?" Dead serious, Jim was no longer the playboy.

"I overheard a conversation," Kay said. "Is it true?"

"Yes, it's true. Mac unwittingly did a lens implant on a cataract patient, not realizing that the lens was a counterfeit. Unfortunately, the lens gave the patient visual problems immediately and the suit resulted. The lens had been purchased by Mac's regular supplier and sold to him."

"Is that why he's in Haiti, paying his penance?"

"Kay, wait a minute. Mac was an innocent."

"Then how come that lens wasn't checked out before it was implanted?"

"I don't have the answer to that. The point is that a copycat lens is also a flawed lens, like a lot of other copycat products."

For a moment Kay wondered exactly what Jim's role was in all this. Without any I.D. from him, she couldn't possibly trust him. She didn't think Mary Ellen would get mixed up with anyone unscrupulous. But then again, how would she know?

It was shortly after midnight when they returned to the hotel. Jim tiptoed down the hall to his room, a finger over his lips as he winked at Kay. Kay opened and closed the door to her room as quietly as she could.

Seconds later, there was a knock at her door. Thinking it was Jim and that he had forgotten something, she opened it without question. Dr. MacDonald walked past her into the room.

"Why are you making my life difficult?" he asked.

"What's the trouble? Didn't I beat the curfew?"

"I told you I have to count noses around here."

"So?"

"And lips, too," he said, his mouth slowly coming down to meet hers.

His arms tightened around her as if he never wanted to let go. She willed herself to be passive, but in that, too, failed.

"Put your arms around my neck," he whispered. Hypnotized, she followed orders. Her defenses dissolved into nothingness.

Suddenly, she didn't care. She opened her eyes to look at him. He smiled lazily at her. A special, sweet ache within her begged to be answered. Of course, she was enjoying being in his arms. Whatever was she thinking? Wake up, Kay, he's a suspect. He might be in charge of a full blown smuggling operation here.

"What do you want from me?" Her lips quivered as she tried vainly to control her racing emotions.

"To help you before you make the biggest mistake of your life."

Help from what? Did he really think that she and Jim . . .? No, it was too silly to consider. The attaché case? He never mentioned it.

He touched her lips lightly with his. "Think about what I said."

She remained standing after he left, a nubbin of uneasiness in the pit of her stomach she didn't want to think about.

* * * *

Mac mused over his encounter with Kay. *It would have been pointless to ask her about the attaché case. She'd deny it as she had before, even if I had accused her of possessing it because I found it in her closet. If only I knew what she was up to. Everything in the case was intact, so either she doesn't know the value of the contents or else she's cooking up a scheme of her own. The very fact her door was open when Michel placed the case there indicates she was expecting someone. But who was going to be her caller? How readily she opened the door when I knocked now. Another rendezvous with someone? I'm going to try to help her, but if I only knew where to begin. How can I find the contacts that she's obviously making? Who was lingering outside tonight? Someone from the clinic? If any of the optometric students or Haitians are involved in a copycat operation, I will be the first to step forward to see them prosecuted.*

How can I help Kay, without her fighting me all the way. She doesn't realize she's dealing with people who would shoot first and ask questions afterwards.

The only way I can uncover the truth is to stay close to her and try to remain emotionally detached. That will be the hard part, he thought.

Chapter 4

"Hey, Jean-Pierre, where do you think you're going?" Kay asked.

"Away."

"Since when?"

"Since now."

"What's the rush?"

"A sudden emergency."

"That's as good an excuse as any."

"Do I need a written note from my mother, Kay? I'm not leaving for good. Why the complaint?"

"I've a right to complain. How am I supposed to communicate with the patients?"

His face wrinkled into a scowl. His eyes burned into her. He stroked his forehead lightly, as if erasing the lines that menaced, then feigned a smile and walked away. "Use sign language," he laughed.

She didn't care if he was angry with her. She had a right to be annoyed. She glanced at the line of patients. Then she saw the Haitian. He had just entered the building, disdained the line, and walked towards Kay.

She didn't like the looks of this guy. Shoulder length hair, torn jeans, soiled T-shirt, and an earring dangling from one ear. There were protests from the line of patients who seemed to know where the Haitian was heading.

He continued his way towards her with a swagger. Everything about this man screamed danger. Those in line craned their necks to see what she was going to do.

"You'll have to wait your turn," Kay said, pointing to him to return to the end of the line. She hoped he understood her gesture, if not the English.

"Back, back," Kay shouted, again pointing to where he should be in line. "Get back."

Then he was at her desk. She pulled herself up to her full height. "Get back in line," she commanded in a voice she hoped would brook no argument.

In perfect English, he said, "That's what you think, sister." Before she could respond, he yelled, "I got to see the Doc right away."

"You'll just have to wait your turn. The doctor can only see one person at a time. What makes you think you can barge in here and demand to see Dr. MacDonald?" asked Kay.

"Well, he'll see me, old girl." He gave her a wink, and strode briskly past her down the corridor.

"Hey, I have to fill out a card for you." Kay ran after him and tugged on his shirt.

"I don't need a card," he said, as he started moving toward Mac's cubicle.

"We have to have a patient record."

"You gotta be kidding."

They both had stopped walking and he was trying to release her hand from his shirt.

"I don't need a patient card. Let go of me, so I can see the Doc."

"At least, I'll have to tell the doctor you're here. I need your name."

"He knows my name and when he sees me, he'll know I'm here."

"You can't go in there. The doctor is busy."

"Look, girl, let me spell it out for you loud and clear. All I want is a little Darvon, *vous comprenez*? I've got a headache, see, a big, bad headache and you're making it bigger. Now beat it." He jerked forward unexpectedly, wrenching himself free from Kay's grasp, sending her reeling against the wall.

He yelled at her as if she couldn't understand. "I said I have a headache and the Darvon is the only thing that helps me. Get lost."

"But that doesn't mean you can't wait your turn in line."

Mac's door opened. "Glad to see you," he said to the man, shaking his hand. "I've been wondering where you've been. Come on in. Oh, Kay, this patient will need glasses." He closed the door to his office. Kay motioned the patient to precede her, as she lingered momentarily at the door.

"We ought to hire that girl. She's good," Kay heard the man say.

"I don't want to involve her in this operation," Mac said.

"But, Mac, she kept me away from you, and for a moment I didn't know how I was going to get to you."

"Maybe next time," Mac said, "when you drop in unannounced, you might get rid of the dirty T-shirt and wear a three-piece suit. In other words, look more respectable. She might not hassle you then. And with the money you're making, you should be able to afford at least one suit."

"Can I still wear the earring, Boss?" he asked.

"OK, let's get down to business. Do you have the stuff?"

"Yep, right here."

Kay moved away from the door. She saw Jean-Pierre signalling to her and hurried forward. But her legs wobbled a little. She didn't want to believe, refused to believe what she feared: that Mac was running a drug ring.

"We need a pair of glasses here," Jean-Pierre said, gesturing at the seated patient.

Why was it necessary for Jean-Pierre to leave so suddenly? She was becoming paranoid. She checked out the glasses she had plucked from the box near her and then adjusted them to the patient's face.

Dismissing the patient, she nodded to Jean-Pierre she was ready for the next patient. As she wrote down the information Jean-Pierre dictated, she heard the door open to the examination room and Mac's voice with a, "See you later."

"Right-o, later," and the mysterious Haitian made his way past Kay to the exit.

Kay saw Jean-Pierre look up briefly. A smile of recognition flickered over his face. The Haitian himself acknowledged Jean-Pierre with an almost imperceptible incline of his head.

"Who is that guy, Jean-Pierre?" Kay asked.

Jean-Pierre deliberately turned his attention to the patient before him. "Got all this down, Kay?" he asked.

"Jean-Pierre, I asked you who that Haitian was."

"Which one—in line?"

"Didn't you see him? The one who left Mac's office?"

"No, I'm concentrating on this patient. Kay, please, only this patient, one at a time. I'm through now and you might as well take him over to Dr. Mac."

Was there some kind of a signal exchanged between Jean Pierre and that Haitian? It was quite apparent that the Haitian knew Jean-Pierre.

When she returned to her seat, Kay pulled out a blank 5 x 8 card for the next patient.

"Jean-Pierre, what was his name?"

"That last patient? Why, Kay, don't you know? You wrote the name yourself on the card."

"I'm not talking about that last patient. I'm talking about the guy who had been in with Mac, the one who just left."

Jean-Pierre's face was blank. "I really wouldn't know. Since I didn't see him, how could I tell?"

Of course, he was lying and she knew he was. But why? Unless he's working with that Haitian. Jean-Pierre did say he needed money to go to school.

How was she ever going to find out exactly what Mac was doing?

The rest of the morning became a blur. One part of her tried to assess some of the events that had occurred earlier. The other part was perfunctorily recording information and fitting glasses.

* * * *

Kay was alone after lunch when the first patient appeared at her desk. Fortunately, he spoke a little English. His right eye was bandaged and she thought at first he wanted a change of dressing, but he was pretty upset when she even suggested it.

"No," he said quite emphatically, "I want to see the Doc."

What was his problem? He said he was having a lot of pain in the bandaged eye and he would like some Darvon. Oh no, she thought, not another one.

She walked the patient down the hall and turned him over to Mac. "The patient says he's in pain and wants some Darvon."

"I'll decide what he needs."

Five minutes later, the patient left Mac's room and stopped at Kay's desk. "Bad Doc, no Darvon."

Shortly afterward, Mac followed. "Here's a blank card for you to use. There's nothing wrong with that patient."

"He said he was in pain. Didn't you give him any Darvon?" Kay asked.

"I don't stock Darvon."

Kay looked directly at Mac. "Is that so? That Haitian who had been here this morning to see you . . ."

"Which one?"

"The one with the earring."

"That clown! I remember. What about him?"

"He told me he was here to get some Darvon."

"You must have misunderstood him, but I told you I don't carry Darvon and I don't prescribe it."

"What do you prescribe for pain?"

"There are a lot of painkillers. I can only prescribe what charity donates to the armamentarium here. Besides, how did you know that this last patient was in pain?"

"He told me so."

"It's only an excuse to get some free drugs."

"But he had had an eye injury."

"That's what he said."

Kay stared in disbelief. Is this the compassionate doctor she had heard so much about? "His eye was bandaged."

"He wasn't treated here for an eye injury."

"Is that why you wouldn't do anything for him?"

"Before I answer that, let me ask you if your eye course included First Aid 101?"

"Of course not." Was he laughing at her?

"Well, if you had scrutinized that bandage and seen how it was wound around his head and over his ear, you'd know it was a homemade job. There was nothing wrong with his eye. He never had sustained any injury to it. There was no foreign body and the eye is a healthy eye and provides excellent vision. This guy just thought he'd get some free drugs."

"Then what about that other man, the one with the earring? Don't you think a man like that is dangerous?" Kay asked.

"You're reading too many spy novels these days."

"The guy sashays in here as if he owns the place, asks for Darvon which you don't have, and you don't think that's dangerous?"

"Hardly."

"He complained to me he had a headache and wanted some Darvon," Kay said.

"What's dangerous about that?"

"He bucked his place in line, gave me a rough time because he wanted to see you. Do you know anything about him? Where does he come from?"

"Around here."

"If he asks for Darvon and you say you don't carry it, what exactly was he after?"

"Who knows?"

"So if you didn't have any Darvon, what did you give him?"

"Generic aspirin. You sure have a hang-up about that guy," Mac said, walking away.

Mac reflected for a few minutes while awaiting the next patient. That crazy Henri. He's going to get all of us in trouble unless he tones down that act of his. He has got to learn to stop asking for Darvon. Too damn suspicious.

Mac opened the small package Henri had given him. Only one pair of copycat lenses this time. But without a set of real ones, there was no basis for comparison.

At her desk, Kay realized there were few people she felt she could trust at the clinic. If only she could phone Willoughby, but he hadn't given her a number. Besides, he would probably laugh at her. What she thought was evidence the attaché case—had been taken out of her room. Most likely, Mac doesn't have it stowed in his room. He could have passed the goods on to someone else already.

As for Jean-Pierre, just because he smiled at a suspicious Haitian doesn't make him guilty of anything. Even if she could call Willoughby, she'd have to go into Port-au-Prince and what excuse would she have for that?

"Are you ready to leave for the hotel?" Mac asked, breaking into her reverie. "I want you to come with me tomorrow morning to see if we can persuade Nicole to return. You've been working with her and achieved quite a bit of rapport with her, something we might have to lean on. Nonetheless I can't let that kid's eye go to pot any longer."

"How can you be sure that Nicole will be home?"

"Her grandmother is a voodoo priestess and there's a neighborhood temple nearby; so if there are any rituals being performed on that eye, they'd take place right there."

"Won't you need an interpreter to talk to Nicole's mother and grandmother?"

"An interpreter or a chaperone? Don't you trust me, Kay?" he asked, grinning boyishly.

She wanted to say she didn't trust herself with him. "It's not that, but . . ."

"In answer to your question, I've been here long enough to have picked up a fairly good working knowledge of the patois. I've never had trouble communicating with the natives."

He braked the jeep in front of the hotel. "I'll see you tomorrow then. I hope you don't mind getting up a little earlier than usual. We'll need a good head start in the morning."

. . . .

Kay showered and changed into a pale yellow shift of linen, then went downstairs for dinner. She was surprised to find the dining room empty. She ordered a bowl of Haitian black bean soup and the fresh marinated creviche, the catch of the day, and ate slowly, hoping that others might join her.

She looked up several times during the meal, anticipating that Dr. Mac, Jim, or even Ruth might be dining. No one entered the dining room while she ate. She lingered over a second cup of Haitian coffee.

Ruth and Jim had told her they'd be tied up at the clinic, but Mac didn't mention anything. Even his sarcastic comments would be welcome this evening.

How was she ever going to track down anyone involved in the copycat smuggling?

"Where is everyone tonight?" Kay asked the waiter when he returned to clear away the dinner dishes.

"Some work late at the clinic, some go out for dinner, some go nightclubbing in Port-au-Prince. *Mademoiselle*, lonely?"

"No, no," Kay answered hastily. She wasn't looking for any kind of companionship or trouble.

What better time to search Mac's room! No one around. Perfect. She could be in and out without anyone the wiser. With no Tripwire to help, she'd have to develop her own leads.

She finished her coffee quickly, then stopped at the front desk. "I can't seem to find my key and must have mislaid it. Could I use your passkey? I'll return it to you shortly." The clerk smiled and handed her the key.

Kay tiptoed over to Mac's room, across the hall from hers, and unlocked his door, closing it slightly. She raced back down the steps and laid the passkey on the desk.

Inside Mac's room, her heart pounded like a triphammer. Any minute, she knew, he'd burst in on her. What could she do? What would she say? She almost regretted her action. Now that she was here she'd better hurry before he arrived.

She moved towards the desk. The single drawer was empty except for a half sheet of stationery.

The dresser was next. Her hands were shaking as she pulled open each drawer. The dresser contained only personal items, nothing more.

The last place to search was the closet. She spied the attaché case immediately. Was this the one Mac picked up at the airport and had taken out of her room? She flipped it open. It contained the copycat Ray-Bans, as before, along with the designer frames she had seen before, too. She closed the case and set it aside.

Standing next to it was a smaller case. There was a key

that dangled on a string tied to the handle. The case was not open, so she fitted the tiny key in the lock and, trembling, opened it. Empty. Why would Mac lock this one but leave the attaché case with the fakes unlocked?

She rose to go. Then she heard the loud knocking. She froze, as if in suspended animation. "Kay, open up, it's Mac."

He was back at her door. What could she do now? If she were discovered, she could be arrested for breaking and entering. For all her anguish, what did her efforts get her? Not too much. Nothing more than what she already knew.

The knocking stopped. She sucked in her breath. She dare not move. What would she do if he entered this room? Where could she possibly hide? In desperation she looked at the closet, even under the bed.

She heard his footsteps approach. Then the key in the lock. She positioned herself behind the door and waited, hardly breathing. Suddenly, he withdrew the key, retreated, and headed back downstairs. Now was her chance, her only chance.

She gave a quick check of his room. Everything was in place, undisturbed. She squeezed the doorknob, coaxing the door open, closed it quietly, and scooted across the hall to her own room. Seconds later, Mac was back at her door, rapping and calling her name.

She rubbed her eyes when she opened the door and stifled a yawn.

"Where were you?" he asked.

"Right here."

"You didn't hear me knocking and calling your name?"

"I must have dozed off. I didn't realize how beat I was."

"The desk clerk said you lost your key and needed the passkey to get back in your room."

"I just mislaid it. It was nothing, really."

"Where was it?"

"Here, on the desk."

"And you didn't hear me knock?"

"Afraid not. I was out like a light," she said, and with

that, she closed the door, worried if she said anything further, she'd reveal too much of what she had done.

* * * *

The next morning Kay rose an hour earlier, dressed in her uniform, breakfasted, and was waiting for the doctor in the lobby.

"All set to go?" He surprised her by entering the lobby through the main door. Kay nodded. "I'll be right with you."

The jeep was parked across the street and from her vantage point, Kay commanded a good view of the hotel's entrance. She observed Mac as he left the hotel. His stride was that of a man, strong and purposeful.

He seemed grave and preoccupied with other matters when he joined her, scarcely looking at her. He was wearing navy blue chinos and a light blue and white striped sport shirt that deepened the slate of his eyes.

"Nicole lives near the Kenscoff Gardens," he said. Kenscoff Gardens meant very little to her. She didn't even know where they were. She stared at him after that announcement, not quite knowing what to make of it. He felt her eyes on him and looked at her directly, but only nodded his head, taking her presence for granted. Nothing else was said and they drove on in silence.

The road twisted and turned through forests festooned with vines of crimson blossoms, past the gleaming white architecture of modern villas, the cluttered baroque scrolls, peaked turrets, and pointed arched windows of Victorian mansions, and the thatched roof huts of the poor.

Wherever the road led them, they met a continuous single file of native women, dressed in bright colored cottons, their hips swinging in a loping gait and balancing huge baskets on their heads loaded with fruits and vegetables. Plodding along beside them were their burros, whose panniers were stuffed with heavier produce.

The air was cooler as the jeep climbed further. The

sides of the mountains bore the scars of erosion. At length the jeep stopped in a slight clearing where Dr. Mac pointed out the neighborhood voodoo temple decorated with bizarre symbols. A few feet away from the temple stood a wood frame hut, its walls mud-daubed.

The door was partially open. Dr. Mac rapped and called out, "*Hono.*" From inside came the response of "*Respe.*" He entered, Kay following close behind. Nicole's mother nodded and broke into a grin at their entrance.

She was wearing a lavender kerchief on her head. Her wide-necked blouse and full gathered skirt were in the same hue.

She was a tall and well proportioned black. Her slanted eyes and high cheekbones gave her an Oriental bearing, despite a complexion that was smooth ebony.

Nicole was sitting on the floor, her little hands clutching a doll. Kay noted that it was nothing more than a few sisal hemp fibers coiled in such a way so that the large knot that tied the strands together could be painted with a face.

Nicole smiled immediately when she saw Kay. "Kay-Kay," she uttered spontaneously.

Mac knelt down next to her and aimed a pinpoint shaft of light in her eye. The child backed away. He spoke to her. The light bothered her. She dropped her doll, covering her eyes with both of her hands. Mac muttered an oath. "That's all I need." He pulled the child's hands away from her eyes.

"Kay, give me some help here, will you?"

Kay tried to divert the child's attention, but as soon as the light was aimed at Nicole, she turned her head away.

"Damn it," Mac said, "how am I going to see if this kid's eye is all right?"

Kay scooped up Nicole and sat down with the child in her lap, encircling her protectively with her arms. Gently, she turned Nicole's face towards Mac and held it in that position.

It was then that Kay saw the pair of sunglasses on the floor where Nicole had been sitting. Kay stared. Ray-Ban.

She'd recognize them anywhere. What was a pair of Ray-Bans doing in a place like this? Nicole and her mother were too poor to buy a pair. The very fact that they went to the clinic reflects their need. Unless someone gave the pair to Nicole's mother.

Kay was determined to return here alone and investigate. She didn't know how she'd get back, but she'll have to think of some excuse, something that won't make her own entry suspicious.

"I'm speaking to you, Kay."

"Sorry, Doctor."

"You can put Nicole down. I'm through with the examination."

"Is everything all right?"

"The blood has partially cleared. But I won't be happy till I can get her back to the clinic where I can observe her the next few days."

Then Mac spoke to Nicole's mother. Kay placed the child back on the floor and rose to stand to the side. She watched Mac as he talked. The planes of his face softened while he tried to encourage the mother to return Nicole to the clinic.

Kay listened to him, without understanding. The words rolled off his tongue lazily in a lilting almost singsong fashion. But she didn't need to understand the language to recognize the care and tenderness with which he delivered his plea. This was a far cry from the Dr. Mac she thought she knew.

Mac's voice continued to cajole, wheedle, and coax the mother. He didn't give up. Kay couldn't help but admire him. The health of the child meant something to him. Not once did he falter in his efforts to persuade.

As if on signal ending the conversation, Nicole's mother brought out a small wooden tray, the top of which was covered with a cloth on which three coffee cups rested.

Kay looked questioningly at Mac. "We'll have a cup of

coffee before taking leave, or Nicole's mother will be offended," he said.

Nicole laid her doll down and came over to Kay, shyly touching her hand and looking at Kay to catch her reaction.

"I wish I had something to give her, a little trinket or toy," Kay said.

"Don't get into that habit," Mac said sharply. "We're not going to bribe anyone to come to the clinic. We want them to come to us of their own free will."

They finished their coffee, said good-bye to Nicole and her mother. Kay, on impulse, stooped down and put her arm around the child, kissing her lightly on the cheek.

"Time to go," Mac said impatiently.

Kay straightened up and waved to Nicole. The child withdrew to the safety of her mother's skirts. "Can't we take Nicole with us now?" Kay asked.

"No, it would be too frightening for both mother and daughter. I think the mother will bring her back."

"How can you be so sure?"

"Watching you hug Nicole convinced me."

Kay walked towards the jeep

"We're not taking the jeep," he called. Kay stopped in her tracks, surprised.

"Aren't we going back to the clinic?" she asked.

"I want to take you to some place special first."

They continued to follow the road up the mountains. "Here it is, the Chatelet des Fleurs." Within a frame of mountain green was a floral picture of acres and acres of sweet peas, snapdragons, carnations, gladioli, blue larkspur.

"It's beautiful," Kay said breathlessly.

"You see? I didn't mislead you after all, did I? These flowers are grown for shipment to the U.S. market," he explained.

"What's beyond this road?" Kay asked.

"Haiti's highest mountain—LaSelle. You can see it from here. And over there, near the periphery of the flowers is Kenscoff's fruit and vegetable market. Many of the women we passed today on the road were on their way to sell and exchange their produce. Should we go?" he asked, looking at his watch. "We've spent more time at Nicole's than I originally planned."

Kay took one last look at the profusion of color behind her. Ringed around them were the billowy layers of blue mountain haze. Below them, the road had been split and sundered into the hairpin turns they had traversed earlier.

Mac preceded her, then held out an assisting hand as she tried to negotiate a steep embankment. As his fingers reached hers, his touch electrified her senses, as though a spark passed from him to her. For a moment time stood still for both as he sought her eyes. In his eyes was the recognition of the effect he had on her.

"If Nicole had needed surgery for her accident, what would you have done?" asked Kay, settling into the jeep.

"Taken her to Port-au-Prince."

"I thought your malpractice suit would have prevented that."

"How did you know about the suit?"

"Jim mentioned it," Kay said.

"Jim has a big mouth and hasn't learned yet to keep secrets, which is going to get him in a lot of trouble some day."

"I don't think Jim meant any harm when he told me."

"Did he tell you that I was cleared of any wrongdoing?"

"He inferred that, but didn't go into any detail."

"That's the trouble with the malpractice suit. Even if a doctor is innocent, the notoriety of the trial is what lingers in the public mind."

There was a bit of anger simmering just below the surface. Kay could feel it. It was in the thin line of his mouth and the rising inflection of his voice.

"All that litigation cost me plenty," he continued. "My insurance rates skyrocketed after that."

"What could you do about that—protest?" Kay asked.

"One alternative was to quit surgery." Anger flared momentarily in his eyes.

Why did Ruth tell her that he goes to Port-au-Prince for his surgery? "I don't understand how you can operate then."

"You know, you ask too many questions for just an optician," he said, dismissing her with a smile, as he turned his attention to the road.

The route now carried them further down the mountain. The warmth of the sun was a welcome change from the cooler temperatures and enhanced Kay's own awareness of well-being.

"Did you see that pair of sunglasses Nicole had in her hand?" she asked.

"Vaguely." He seemed totally disinterested, almost bored.

"They were Ray-Ban. I'd recognize them anywhere."

"Good for you."

"Aren't you concerned?"

"Why should I be? Why do you care?"

"Those are expensive glasses."

"So I understand."

His indifferent response puzzled her. Was it to throw her off the trail? Suddenly, she realized she wanted to find evidence that would clear him of any suspicion. She didn't know why. She wasn't quite sure of her own feelings yet. But she wanted to help him, for her sake, too.

"How could Nicole's mother afford a pair of sunglasses like that when she's so very poor?"

"Maybe someone gave them to her."

But who, Kay wondered, and why. Kay knew she must return somehow, some way to Nicole's house to find out the source of the glasses. She'd also have to depend on someone to drive her up there. But what could she use as a pretense for returning to Nicole's?

When they finally arrived at the clinic, Ruth came out to greet Mac, a big smile on her face.

"Don't know what method of persuasion you used,"

she said, "but Nicole is back. She and her mother must have left as soon as you did."

"We stopped at Chatelet des Fleurs instead of returning directly," Mac explained.

Ruth stared at him in disbelief. "Doctor, you mean to say you stopped to smell the flowers when we need you here? You're the only M.D. on duty. Anyway, I put Nicole to bed," Ruth continued, "and taped a fresh bandage over that eye."

"Come now, Ruth, you didn't need me to do that, did you, really?" A sly smile crept over his face.

"I've got her arms back in restraints because she keeps reaching for that eye."

"Very good, Ruth. What would I ever do without you," he said, squeezing her arm. Kay felt the color mounting in her cheeks.

"You feel all right, Kay?" He eyed her critically.

"Sure," she said lightly.

"Your face is quite flushed. That mountain climb might have been too much for you."

"By the way, Kay, Nicole has been asking for you," Ruth said.

Kay hurried off, grateful for an opportunity to escape from Mac's scrutiny.

Kay became alarmed when she saw how frightened the child was, pulling and straining in frustration at her arms, trying to loosen the shackles that bound her. There was no change here.

Kay sat down on the edge of the bed and stroked the child's forehead. What was accomplished after all the hassle? Outside of the fact they got Nicole back to the clinic, she was just as miserable as she had been in the past. One of the Haitian nurses brought Nicole her lunch and freed her arms so she could sit up and feed herself.

Kay left them and went to the fridge to get her own lunch, then walked out slowly to the backyard and sat down at one of the tables. The image of Nicole bothered her. Dr. Mac installed himself next to her.

"You're looking better," he said.

"Doctor," she began, ignoring his comment.

"Mac," he interrupted her. "It's either Mac or Ian. I'll give you a choice." He smiled at her.

"Want to start from the beginning?" he asked.

This time she did not address him. "I'm worried about Nicole."

"Why? She's getting good care."

"It's not that. The restraints on that child are terrifying her again and she is as unhappy as she was when we first put her to bed."

"We got her back here so that we could put her in restraints and keep her hands out of that eye. It's a miracle as it is that the blood had cleared as well as it did."

"Suppose her mother comes to visit and sees her like that. She might carry her off again."

"That's a chance we'll have to take. It's the only way to prevent that kid from putting her finger in her eye. Stop brooding, Kay."

"But she's such a baby."

"All the more reason. How do you explain to a five-year-old why she shouldn't put her fingers in her eye?"

"Well . . ."

"Exactly. When you find the answer to that one, my dear, let me know."

His words jolted her with their bluntness. "Kay," he said softly, as if regretting his brusque tone, "don't look so crushed. Our measures aren't draconian. They're for the good of the child."

Kay finished her sandwich and followed him back into the clinic.

She skipped back to Nicole for a quick peek. Poor little tyke, surrounded by strangers and not understanding what was happening to her.

If only the child's mother could stay with her until her discharge. Of course, that was out of the question.

Kay approached the bed. Nicole stopped whimpering.

"Kay, Kay." Her eyes pleaded with Kay to free her, as she tugged and pulled on the restraints.

Kay spoke to one of the Haitian nurses. Everyone was sympathetic to Nicole, but there really wasn't much they could do to allay the five-year-old's apprehension. Removing the restraints wouldn't help anything, least of all, the injured eye.

Chapter 5

*L*ater, as Kay walked down the hall to her station, she despaired over Nicole's plight. Sure, Mac's the doctor and knows what's best for the patient, but Nicole needs something more than just the medical prescription. A wave of irritation swept over Kay because he called the shots but made no provisions for the other aspect, the psychological one, for the child's health care.

She looked up for an instant when she heard her name called. There's that jerk with the earring. He's back. The nerve of that guy! She watched him as he skirted the line of waiting patients, waved briefly to her, matched with a big smile, and made a beeline for Mac's office. "Oh no, you don't, not this time," Kay said out loud. She shot past her station. "I'll be right back," she shouted to Jean-Pierre, as she raced to cut off the familiar intruder.

"Do you have another headache or is it still the Darvon you're after?" Kay challenged.

"I don't know what you're talking about," he said, taken aback by her sudden spurt of boldness.

"Really? Well, let me refresh your memory. The doctor doesn't have Darvon and never did, so what's your excuse this time for breaking through the line?"

"Too bad you're such a hothead. I could use somebody like you," he said.

"You're hiding something and I want to know what it is."

"Why don't you run along like a good little girl and take care of those patients. You're creating a gridlock down there."

"I'm sorry, but you're not going to see the doctor," Kay said and planted herself in front of Mac's door.

"You don't want me to get rough, do you?" he asked, trying to push her aside.

"You're good at that, aren't you? I don't know where you get the idea that your need to see Dr. MacDonald is any more urgent than all those people waiting patiently in line."

"Because I have something to give and they don't."

"Such as?"

"Wouldn't you like to know?" He shoved her aside, knocked twice on the examination door, and entered without waiting for an answer. "Mac, I'll leave it right here. Forgot to bring it last time."

Kay heard an, "OK" from within. The messenger closed the door behind him and winked at her. "Now that didn't hurt, did it?" he asked Kay. She stared at him.

"Cheer up," he said, "things are getting better. I won't be around for awhile."

"Is that a promise?" Kay asked.

"Trying to get rid of me, eh?" Kay turned her back on him and returned to her station.

"Come on, Kay, we got patients piling up," Jean-Pierre said. "I don't know why you bother with that guy in the first place."

"Because he's got some kind of a racket going and I'd like to know what it is. Why does he have seniority status that he feels every time he comes to the clinic, he can just ram his way through?"

"As long as he's not dangerous," Jean-Pierre replied, "what difference does it make?"

"How do you know he's not dangerous?"

"Kay, count me out of this. All I want to do now is to get this line of patients moving."

"All right. We'll talk later."

• • • •

After the first six patients had been attended to, there was a lull in the routine while Jean-Pierre and Kay waited for Dr. Mac to catch up with them.

"Nicole is back, I hear," Jean-Pierre said.

"Yes, she is, but it's so pitiful to see her tug on those restraints."

"Not much the doctor can do about that."

"Jean-Pierre, I was thinking. Would you drive me to Nicole's house after work?"

"Sure," the Haitian said, "but do you know the way?"

"I think I do."

"Then what, after we get there?"

"I'm going to need you as interpreter. Nicole had a doll she was very attached to and I thought that if I brought it back to her and could lay it next to her, she might be more content until she has to be discharged."

"Nothing ventured, nothing gained. We'll talk later."

• • • •

There were few conflicts in the afternoon as Kay led a steady stream of patients down the hall to Dr. Mac's examination room and he in turn delivered those who needed glasses. Kay worked, inspired with the idea of bringing a little joy into the lonesome child's life.

After hours, Kay wasted no time in leaving the clinic, so she and Jean-Pierre could make their getaway unseen. Kay wanted to avoid any questions Dr. Mac might ask if he saw her.

The drive up the mountains seemed to take forever. There were moments when Kay thought she had given Jean-Pierre the wrong directions. Then she began to have second thoughts about the soundness of her idea. Suppose her brainstorm didn't work and Nicole's mother refused to give her the doll. How could Kay persuade her otherwise. If the mother doubted her intentions, would she be able to allay such suspicions?

Outside of the fact that the mother knew she worked at the clinic, there was no other way Kay could prove her sincerity and desire to help Nicole.

"How much farther is it?" Jean-Pierre asked, interrupting her train of thought.

"I don't know. I was sure we should have been there already. At dusk, everything looks so different. I hope we're not lost."

"How can you get lost on an island?"

"There it is," Kay said, pointing, "over there, by the voodoo temple." They parked the car and approached the house.

Jean-Pierre rapped lightly on the door, calling out, "*Hono.*"

Nicole's mother opened it, recognized Kay, and replied with her greeting of, "*Respe,*" gesturing to both of them to enter.

Inside, near the entrance, Kay saw the sunglasses. They were spilling out of two open boxes on the floor. There was no attempt to conceal them. Was this poor woman caught in a bootleg operation? Whoever dropped them off here must be planning to stop by later, maybe.

Momentarily, Kay forgot why she had come and knelt down to examine the sunglasses. Just as she had suspected, Ray-Bans. All of them.

Then she heard Jean-Pierre's voice. He pointed in her direction, or was it the sunglasses he was talking about?

Puzzled, Kay watched him. He wasn't talking about a doll. She was sure about that. They're discussing something else. They're much too serious, both of them.

The only word Kay recognized exchanged between the two of them was "*Non.*" Nicole's mother spat out the word in protest, and stamped her foot for emphasis. Kay didn't understand Creole, but that "*Non*" had nothing to do with a doll.

Without further ado, the mother brought the doll over to Kay.

"Jean-Pierre, can you ask her where she got all those sunglasses?"

"I thought we came here for the doll. You got the doll, now let's go."

"Jean-Pierre, please ask her where she got the sunglasses."

"I can tell you she's too poor to buy them." She was right. He had spoken to her about them. "Besides, Kay, what would she want with so many of them?"

"Can't you ask anyway?" Kay persisted.

"Look, Kay, we came here for the doll. Do you want the doll or do you want the sunglasses? If I had known what your real motive was in coming here, I never would have agreed to bring you."

"Just ask one more time, Jean-Pierre, then I won't bring it up again."

The mother's face tightened up immediately when Jean-Pierre resumed his questioning.

"I asked her if she was expecting someone to pick up those glasses. First she said maybe, then she said she didn't know. She said she has done nothing wrong. She has to make a living for herself and her daughter."

Could she trust Jean-Pierre? Was he really asking the questions she told him to? If Jean-Pierre were in on this deal, he could profit nicely and he had once said he could use a lot of money to go to school.

Jean-Pierre turned to her. "Satisfied?"

It was the way he said it that bothered Kay. Far from being satisfied, Kay promised herself she was going to do her own investigative work.

Back in the car, Jean-Pierre said, "You certainly are interested in those sunglasses."

"Aren't you?" Kay asked.

"What good would it do me, if I were?"

"But doesn't it strike you as odd that Nicole's mother has all those sunglasses?"

"Not really. She's probably going to take them to the Iron Market to sell. What you don't know, Kay, is that smuggled consumer goods have been flooding the market for some time. As much as half of all the goods being sold on the street here are contraband."

"I guess I didn't expect to find anything like those glasses in these surroundings."

"A lot of consumer stuff like bikes and even rice and flour are stolen from the U.S., then smuggled into Haiti and offered for sale at a rock bottom price."

"But those glasses might not be from the U.S., but to the U.S."

"From where then?"

"Maybe Brazil."

"Then, if you think they're from Brazil, what are they?" Jean-Pierre asked.

"Copycat glasses."

"So what if they are? They aren't hurting anyone."

"They could be. Someone in the States, thinking he found a bargain in Ray-Ban sunglasses might not know that the lenses are inferior and don't protect him from the sun."

"How can you tell these are copycats when you didn't even check out the lenses?"

"For one thing, the trade name is misspelled, Ray-Ban with two *N*s."

"Where did you learn so much about copycat glasses?"

"I used to model sunglasses like the Ray-Ban."

"Oh. But you're not a model now." A pause followed. "Are you an investigative journalist?"

"I'm an optician."

"So you say."

Almost blew her cover. Got to learn to keep her mouth shut.

Jean-Pierre parked in front of the clinic. "I'll wait here for you while you run in and give Nicole the doll."

"That won't be necessary. I see Ruth's car over there. I'll catch a ride back to the hotel with her. I'll see you Monday. Thanks again, Jean-Pierre, for your help."

She waved him off and went into the clinic, walking down the corridor to Nicole's room. The child was asleep. Kay took the doll and slipped it gently under Nicole's arm. She stirred briefly but didn't open her eyes, and Kay tiptoed away.

Only one Haitian nurse was on duty. Strange, there was no sign of Ruth anywhere. Kay asked the nurse if she knew where Ruth was and the girl said that Ruth and Dr. MacDonald had gone out together.

Now what to do? Should she start walking back to the hotel, hoping she'd be picked up by a member of the staff, or should she remain at the clinic.

The two optometrists and Jim had gone to Petionville for dinner and they'd have to return this way to get to the hotel, but who knows how late that would be. Even as a creature of impulse, she reasoned, walking at this hour would be foolhardy and the possibility of meeting anyone from the clinic was remote.

She closed the door to the ward room, blocking the illumination from spilling into the rest of the clinic, and retraced her steps. The front part of the clinic was dark and foreboding. Now that the ward was cut off from the rest of the clinic, the building had an empty sound. There were creaks and groans she never noticed in the daytime. The chirps and buzzing of insects outside were louder than usual, too.

She groped her way past her desk, then over to Mac's examination room. The door was closed. She jiggled the knob and to her surprise, the door was unlocked and swung ajar with little effort.

The lights from a passing car struck the instruments on display. The shadow of the slit lamp microscope appeared as a medieval instrument of torture on the adjacent wall.

She felt along the wall for the light switch, flipped it on, and sat down at the small desk in the room, opening a drawer. Nothing too important in it: a stethoscope, blood pressure cuff, an ophthalmoscope, and some scratch pads, all blank.

She heard the footsteps first, but, determined, she continued to tug on the handle of a cabinet near the desk.

"Looking for something?" He was leaning against the door jamb, his arms folded across his chest, his face impassive.

She froze. Her mind raced to grab at some feasible reason for her presence. "I merely wanted to see . . . uh . . . where you examine the patients." She spoke as evenly as possible.

"At this hour?"

"I have a headache and thought I could find something to take." She felt like a child caught with her fingers in the cookie jar, throwing out one excuse after another with the hope that if he rejected one, another would satisfy.

"You mean, like Darvon, the Darvon I don't prescribe?" His eyes narrowed. "I gather you're disappointed in what you see."

"Why should I be?" she asked, wondering what he was up to.

He lifted one shoulder indifferently. "Because there's nothing here, of course." His voice reverberated in the room and his delivery seemed a little slow, dangerously so.

Excuse making was not her forte. Neither was acting. She stood there, not knowing how to respond.

"Would you like to see what's in that cabinet—that you seem to think contains a mysterious potion?"

"If it's not too much trouble," she said.

He smiled. "My pleasure. I do this all the time, especially, during evening hours." He crossed over to the cabinet and unlocked it. "There, take a look, a really good look, if you think there's something in there you must see and must have."

She peered at the array of bottles.

"There's nothing mysterious and I'm not trying to hide anything. I do have some drugs."

"Drugs?" she asked, trying not to sound too interested.

"A few. Sedatives, antibiotics . . ."

"Amphetamines?" she asked.

"Is that what you're interested in?" he asked, caught by surprise. A member of his own staff involved in contraband goods and drugs? Why weren't these volunteers screened better? What was she mixed up in and who was she working for? He knew she would deny everything, if questioned.

She looked at him as if he had uttered an obscenity. "I mean an aspirin . . . for a headache."

"What I have here," he was saying, avoiding looking at her, "is whatever might prove helpful to the patients, if needed. We keep things locked up because it would be too easy for the workers and others to help themselves."

Kay wondered if Mac was the only one who had the key to that lock. But she was leery about asking.

Mac studied Kay carefully. He wished that he could figure her out. Worried that something might have happened to her or that she was ill, he had borrowed the hotel's passkey to get in her room. There wasn't a single clue to tell him where she had gone or if someone had even kidnapped her, as farfetched as that was.

"Mac did you find her? Oh, pardon me," Ruth said, as she looked from Mac to Kay. Kay was almost grateful for the interruption.

"I'm going back to take a look at my patient," Mac said, excusing himself.

It was Ruth's voice, Ruth's face, but it bore little resemblance to the R.N. Kay knew at the clinic. Ruth was wearing a strapless silk organza of shimmery silver which tapered to a generous leggy slit. Her hair was swept up into a modified beehive, adorned with three scatter pins of rhinestones. Her makeup was perfect. That's why Kay didn't recognize her. At the clinic Ruth never wore any cosmetics. Kay had to admit Ruth was transformed into a very attractive woman.

"Do you realize we have been scouring the countryside for you," Ruth asked angrily. "Well?" she demanded impatiently, "what do you have to say for yourself? We've spent a couple of hours looking for you."

"I'm sorry," Kay said meekly.

"You ought to be. Mac and I were going out, and when you didn't show up for dinner and didn't answer your door, Mac was sure something had happened to you, although I don't know why he was worried about you. You sure look old enough to me to take care of yourself. This is the second time we've been at the clinic, searching. You weren't here before. We drove all around, everywhere, not even knowing in what direction you might have gone."

"I went back to Nicole's house."

"What kind of a wild goose chase was that?"

"Nicole was very frightened and I thought that if I could bring her one of her toys from home, she'd feel better, comforted with something familiar to her."

"That makes a lot of sense, doesn't it? We're wasting time and risking our necks looking for you in No Man's Land and you're gallivanting off in the wild blue yonder on the trail of what?"

"A doll. I wasn't gallivanting. Jean-Pierre took me and brought me back to the clinic."

"Then why didn't he drive you to the hotel, too?"

"I saw your car and assumed you would be here and I

could ride with you, so I told him not to wait. The nurse on duty told me you had left with Dr. MacDonald."

"Somebody mention my name?" Dr. Mac said. "I just looked in on Nicole. She's sleeping like an angel with her doll. Where did she ever get that?"

"Our eager beaver here is responsible for that," Ruth said. "She went back to Nicole's after work to get the doll, then found out she didn't have a ride back to the hotel because everyone was gone."

Kay bristled. Ruth's description made her feel like a wayward teenager.

"How did you get to Nicole's?" Dr. Mac asked.

"Jean-Pierre took me and brought me back, but I thought someone at the clinic would be going to the hotel, so I told him to go on without me."

"Still the creature of impulse, aren't you?" he accused. He was inviting an argument, but Kay refused to bite. "When are you going to grow up? I was all set to call out the Marines." Did she have to be ashamed because she performed an act of kindness?

"Mac, you haven't forgotten about our date, have you?" Ruth asked.

"No, I haven't. Why don't you go out in the jeep and wait for me?" Ruth looked at him questioningly. "You heard me, Ruth, I'll be along shortly."

"I worried about you when you weren't at the hotel," he said softly.

"I'm not a child." She was angry he was going out with Ruth.

"Then stop acting like one."

That stung. Not once did he praise her for showing compassion for little Nicole. "You don't have to stay and fuss over me."

"And you tell me how the devil you're going to get back to the hotel if I don't drive you."

"I wouldn't dream of ruining your evening, Doctor."

"Wouldn't you, though? Next time tell someone at the

clinic where you're going to be. It will be a lot easier on everyone." Could he ever believe her, believe that her trip to Nicole's was the innocent errand to get the doll and nothing else? How much still lay untold?

"I thought something had happened to you," he said.

"Am I to be flattered by your concern?"

"Kay, listen to me. It would be a lot easier if you'd stop lying and tell me the truth."

"What makes you think I'm lying?"

"I recovered my attaché case in your room."

"Which proves what?"

"You denied you had it when I asked you."

"Michel must have placed it in my room by mistake."

"That part is right, but Michel told me your door was unlocked, as if you were expecting someone. Who was that someone?"

"I don't have to answer that."

"I want to help you because I think you're mixed up in something you have no right to be. Who are you really, Miss Thompson? And what are you doing here in Haiti? Are you an investigative reporter?"

"I'm getting a little tired of reiterating that I am not an investigative reporter."

"Who else has been asking questions?"

"Jean-Pierre."

"Really? Interesting. Why did you come to Haiti—the truth."

"Because I wanted to help the Haitians."

"Mac, are you coming or are you going to spend the rest of the night in the clinic?" Ruth barged in on them.

"I'm coming right now. We'll drop Kay off at the hotel first."

As he drove up to the hotel entrance, Mac said, "You can probably get an aspirin from the desk clerk; that is, if you still have that headache."

Kay got out without a word to either of them. It wasn't till she was in her room that she realized how hungry she was and that she hadn't had dinner yet. She showered, changed into a pair of green jeans with a green polka dotted shirt, and went downstairs to the dining room.

"I hope you're still serving dinner," Kay said to one of the waiters.

"For you, yes," he said with a mock bow.

Kay ordered a bowl of Haitian bean soup and a salad. As she ate, her thoughts turned to Mac. She knew she shouldn't care if he went out with Ruth, but she did. Was it her imagination or was his manner towards her subdued? Even tonight when she faced him in his examination room, she expected him to unleash a rage that would shake the rafters. Instead, he spoke to her with concern. There seemed to be a change in him, too, when the two of them had gone to Nicole's the other day and then stopped off at Kenscoff Gardens. But otherwise, what a wasted day! She had learned nothing about the sunglasses in Nicole's house, and Mac had accused her of lying.

Well, tomorrow she was going to the beach with Jim and looked forward to that, although Jean-Pierre had told her not to expect too much; that that particular beach was coarse and brown. Its only advantage, he said, was that it was the closest beach to the hotel.

. . . .

Kay rose early and opened up her louvered shutters. The sun, though far from having reached its zenith, was already warm, and yes, comforting, Kay thought, with the promise of a pleasant day at the beach.

She dressed in a bikini of persimmon, slipped into a terrycloth cover-up and went downstairs for a quick breakfast, then returned to her room to get a few things together in a canvas beach bag.

She had zipped everything in there, cast an eye around the room to see if she forgot anything, when there was a knock at the door. She opened it, anticipating Jim, but instead Dr. MacDonald stood there, a sheepish grin on his face. He was wearing light blue jeans and a white T-shirt.

"Aren't you going to invite me in?"

"Where's Jim?" asked Kay.

"He was detained at the clinic and asked me to take you." He pushed his way into the room. "What do you need Jim for when you've got me?"

"But I just saw him yesterday and he reminded me of our date today."

"Don't you believe me?"

"I'm not going with you," she stated firmly.

"Are you trying to make me jealous?"

"Why should I?" asked Kay. "I've told you that I didn't come to Haiti looking for romance. Evidently, you still don't believe me."

"If I said I did, would you go with me?"

"No."

"Are you afraid of me?"

She turned her face away from him then.

"Kay," he said softly and walked over to her, his hand tilting her face towards him. "Afraid that I might make love to you?" She retreated slightly.

He reached out and slowly pulled her towards him. Tenderly, he kissed her. She pushed herself away from him forcibly.

"Don't try to fool me. You like this as much as I do." His mouth descended on hers once again. He set her emotions tingling and she didn't care this time as she wound her arms around his neck and shamelessly responded. What was there about this man that he could so easily ignite that spark of passion within her?

Gently, he pushed her arms away. "I think we better head for the beach, don't you, or we might not get there?"

. . . .

The road spun around sunlit mountains as it began its descent. The sky had become a crystalline blue. Jim had told her that the beach was only a half hour's drive from the hotel, so when Kay looked at her watch and saw they had been riding for over an hour, she became concerned.

"Are you lost, Doctor?"

"Still don't trust me, do you?"

She wanted to say she didn't trust herself with him.

"We should be there soon," he said, smiling, and reaching for her hand.

They arrived at the little village of Petit Goave, passing by a forest of breadfruit, magnolias, palms, and seagrape.

"Over there is Habitation Leclerc." Mac pointed beyond the forest. "The most luxurious resort ever! This whole area used to be the estate of Pauline Bonaparte, Napoleon's sister. Leclerc was her married name. There are villas, pools, tennis courts, restaurants. You name it. Every convenience that a tourist can imagine."

He parked the jeep near a small store that was adjacent to a dock, removing a picnic basket from the rear of the vehicle. He must have really plotted this well in advance to get a lunch ready on such short notice, Kay thought. His deviousness amused her.

Mac seemed very familiar with the place; and the man who rented speedboats greeted him as a long lost son, embracing him in a powerful bear hug.

"A friend of yours?" Kay asked, when they left the store.

"Yes. Maurice and I go way back. He's a little short of boats today, so one of his men will drop us off, then return later, freeing the boat for others."

Did Maurice use his boats to bring in or transport copycat glasses? Mortified, Kay realized she didn't know the man and already suspected him of being part of a smuggling ring.

There were a couple of outboard runabouts bobbing in the water. "We're getting the motor sailer," Mac said, as he led the way.

Kay hesitated. "Is it safe?" she asked.

"Of course, it's safe. Maurice wouldn't rent us a boat that's going to sink."

"Why does it have a motor and a sail if it's so safe?"

"Spoken like a true landlubber. Ordinarily, we'd use the sail first, but since Maurice wants his boat back quickly, and I want to get to the beach just as quickly, we'll use the power auxiliary. Stop worrying. Besides, our trip will take only fifteen minutes."

"A lot can happen in fifteen minutes."

"Yes, I suppose it can," he said, appraising her, as he took her hand and helped her into the boat.

"Is Maurice only in the tourist business?" Mac looked at her sharply. There was something there in his eyes. It was fleeting, but she caught the expression. "I mean does he do anything else with these boats?"

"Like what, for instance?"

"I mean . . ."

"You don't know what you mean. No more questions till later, OK?"

The Haitian pilot grunted acknowledgement when they boarded. They sat on seats that were no more than wooden planks stretched laterally across the width of the small craft. Mac sat with his arm around her. "Wouldn't want anything to happen to you after I took such pains in planning everything today."

Just as she thought. Kay turned her face away to hide her smile. "Whatever happened to Jim? You never did tell me."

"Jim? Oh yeah, Jim. He had quite a few things that came up suddenly at the clinic."

It was impossible to hear anything else over the din of the motor so Kay followed with interest the filigree patterns of foam the boat was weaving in its wake on the glassy surface of the water.

Minutes later, the boatman steered his craft into a secluded cove. Mac thanked the driver and helped Kay climb out.

"Now wasn't this worth it all?" he asked.

Before her lay a beach of sugar white sand rimmed by a wide band of emerald water blending into aquamarine, then into ultramarine, finally melding into an expanse of electric blue that extended farther away from the shore.

There was no one around. The coconut palms that bordered the beach scarcely rustled their fronds. Only the gentle lapping of placid waves marred the tranquility of the scene.

"Guard this with your life," Mac said, grinning and handing the picnic basket to her. She nodded, not daring to speak, afraid to break the spell. But she, too, was under a spell, cast by the sun and Mac, standing at the edge of the beach in his trunks. His body could have been of any shape or proportion and it still would have delighted her.

There wasn't an ounce of fat on him. His thighs were hard, muscular; his hips, firm and narrow. His stomach was taut and flat as a pancake.

He turned and waved to her. "Hurry up, before the water cools off." He plunged into the surf, then whipped around to observe her.

He saw her drop the terrycloth cover-up and pause, uncertain as to what to do next. Her hair was caught up in a ponytail and tied with a piece of persimmon yarn, making her appear so much more bewitching. She tucked some arrant strands of hair into a swimming cap.

He had known the pleasure of her lips long before they had kissed. He knew the curves and dips of her body long before he would ever make love to her. Desire rushed through his veins. He felt his inhibitions suddenly dissolve and dove into the water with a vengeance, slicing effortlessly with long, easy reaches of the crawl. The water responded to his movements with the merest of agitation.

Kay watched him with admiration. Now it was her turn. She waded gingerly into the water, almost fearing to tread lest she flaw its surface with her footprints. The water was delightfully warm. She dunked herself a couple of times, then propelled through the water with the side stroke.

How long she swam, she didn't know. There was such a suspension of time that it could have been hours for all she knew or cared. She rolled over on her back and floated contentedly, dreamily gazing up at the sky which was streaked here and there with wisps of clouds.

The feeling of peace that engulfed her was addictive. She could languish like this forever. A shadow fell over her, followed by a grinning face.

"Hello. Remember me?"

What had he been doing while she was swimming? His hair was dry. How long had he been out of the water and why?

"I've been waiting for you," he said. "You didn't think I was going to let you swim alone, did you?"

"What have you been doing?" she asked.

"Getting the food ready."

She had wondered where he had gone.

"How about some lunch?"

Was it that late already, she thought. She looked at him without comprehending.

"I've got the table set," he said.

Kay paddled towards shore. Dr. Mac led her to where he had spread a blanket, and on top of that, a tablecloth.

"We have chicken, French bread, brie, and a bottle of chablis, *mademoiselle*."

"I didn't realize I was so famished," Kay said, toweling her hair and face.

He opened a second blanket for them on which to sit. "You know," he said, as he poured the wine, "I've often been curious if a girl who wears a bikini can really swim."

"And are you still curious?" Kay asked, gnawing on a drumstick.

"Not any more, but the surgeon general should have a

warning label placed on all bikinis, that they're hazardous to one's health."

"Hazardous for whom?"

"For me, sets me on fire," he said, scooting over to her, and wrapping his arms around her.

"Let's finish eating," Kay said.

"Who can think of food at a time like this? You don't want to eat now, do you?" He took the piece of French bread out of her hand and out of her reach.

His arms tightened around her. The kiss that followed was brief, but tender. Kay moved away from him.

"Why are you avoiding me?" he asked.

"Coming here on a picnic with you is hardly avoidance." Could she tell him how much she enjoyed being in his arms and how she wanted him to kiss her and hold her? How she wanted to forget about everything and everyone and just be with him? But she was afraid, afraid that her body would betray her and she might say something she'd regret later.

"I think there are things you want to tell me," he said, reading her mind, "but are afraid to, aren't you?" Once again, their lips met, this time longer and with more passion.

"If you're in trouble, Kay, perhaps I can help you, but I have to know everything. Let me help you. I want you to trust me. Are you here on some kind of journalistic assignment?"

"I'm not going to keep reiterating that I'm not an investigative reporter."

"Then why keep denying that you are? Why have you come here, Kay? Please, just explain. The truth now."

"What possible motive could I have in lying about being an optician?"

"I can think of several, none of them particularly pleasant. You're hiding something from me, Kay, and eventually, I'll find out what it is. You're putting on some sort of act, of that much I'm sure. The only thing I don't know is why you're doing it."

"You have no right to make such accusations."

"No logical reasons, maybe. Let's begin all over again, shall we?"

"About time."

"Are you and Jim lovers?"

"What in the world has that got to do with anything?"

"I think for a lot of reasons you've been trying hard, very hard to appear as something you really aren't."

"Doctor, is this what you brought me out to this lonely stretch of beach to ask me? Then it's time to take me home. Now."

"Your show of outrage isn't too convincing." Mac couldn't decide whether she was really an optician or just about the most beautiful liar he had ever met. He placed his hand on her shoulder and she promptly removed it.

"You can't leave without our boatman," he said, enjoying her frustration, "unless you want to swim for it."

"Very funny." She stood up, hoping to catch a glimpse of the boat that would take them back. She was disgusted. He brought her out here for a little romance, to butter her up so she would give him some information. Nothing could kill a romantic feeling more than knowing you're being set up. Talk about lying! Why did he lie to her about doing surgery in Port-au-Prince?

"You really don't trust me, do you," he said. "I wonder why."

"Do I have to remind you that you've thought the worst about me from the moment we met?"

"I plead guilty," he said, in his best conciliatory manner. "Sit." He pulled her down to him. "Kay, listen to me. There's a lot you don't understand."

"No kidding."

"Listen to me, please. Your mixing in now can cause some very real problems."

"You want me to answer questions, OK, then ask the questions. Let's get this over with."

"Kay, believe me, when I say this hurts me more than it

does you. How much of a payoff are you getting for those phony lenses?"

"Phony lenses? What phony lenses?"

He wanted to excuse her, to protect her, even before he knew what she was hiding. "You know the kind, say, an ophthalmic surgeon would be using after a cataract procedure, for an implant."

"I don't know what you're talking about."

"On the contrary, I think you know everything there is to know about payoffs, buying favors."

"Our friend is back," Kay said, the noise of the oncoming speedboat muffling her words.

. . . .

The drive to the hotel began quietly, each reticent about speaking to the other. Kay wanted to break the silence, but she groped helplessly for words that didn't come.

"You're angry," he said, glancing impassively at her. She dared not answer. Her instincts compelled her to resist.

Neither spoke until they reached the hotel. "I've never been so wrong about a woman before," Mac said, bringing her hand to his lips. "Have dinner with me tonight and prove to me otherwise." He bent towards her, his lips lightly touching hers, at first; but then insisting, demanding as before. Despite her irritation with him, she knew she would.

"I'll be in the dining room, waiting for you." He released her.

Kay showered and dressed casually in a linen chemise of fawn. There were too many gray areas about Mac that were unsettling. She suspected he was trying to unmask her, force her into a confession, of what she didn't know. Tripwire, perhaps?

He was seated at a table in the center of the floor. "I already ordered Chateaubriand bearnaise for two, a salad, souffle glace, au grand Marnier, and coffee. How does that sound?" He looked to her for approval. "Hungry?"

"Starved."

"So am I," he said, grinning at her.

The meal was delicious. His affable mood was contagious as he bantered with her.

"You can't leave Haiti without seeing the Citadelle," he said. "I won't let you."

"What is it?"

"I'll tell you only if you'll let me take you there."

Kay smiled at him, but said nothing.

"If I promise to behave myself, will you go?" He looked directly at her, his eyes steady and unblinking.

Was he throwing her a challenge?

"Next Sunday, a week from today? I have to push my advantage," he said.

"But what is it? You still haven't told me."

"Briefly, the Citadelle is a fortress built by Henri Christophe, once president of northern Haiti, to hold the French at bay."

"Oh." She tried to assess his motives.

"What's it going to be? Yes or no?"

"Yes," she replied easily.

The waiter returned to fill their cups. They were lingering over their coffee when Ruth entered the dining room.

"Do you know I've been looking all over for you, Mac?"

"Is there some kind of emergency at the clinic?" he asked.

"Must there always be an emergency for me to see you?" She flicked an angry glance in Kay's direction.

"Ruth, cut the histrionics, will you? We'll talk later."

"You bet your bottom dollar we're going to talk later." Turning to Kay, she said, "And where have you been all day?"

"We were at the beach," Kay said innocently.

"Oh you were, were you?" Her eyes snapped back to Mac. "You're the one who always tells the staff to inform others where they are. Then you can't even follow your own orders, Doctor."

"Ruth, would you mind keeping your voice to a low roar? Everyone is looking at us."

"I don't care who's looking at us. You're the doctor around here and I should know where you are."

As soon as she finished her coffee, Kay excused herself.

"When you can't stand the heat, get out of the kitchen," Ruth said scornfully.

"I have some letters to write," Kay said.

"I'm sure you do," Ruth replied.

Once in her room, Kay reached for the stationery in the desk drawer and remembered she forgot to stop downstairs for a couple of extra sheets when she heard a low, indistinct hum, human, but unintelligible. It rippled into an angry undertone and finally grew into the heated voices of Mac and Ruth as they climbed the stairs and walked past her room.

A door slammed. Kay held her breath, listening. She slipped out into the hall. The accusations and insinuations that filled the air stopped her cold.

"Ruth, for heaven's sakes, be reasonable."

"You be reasonable. You and I were a winning combo until that DuBarry came along. You're making an absolute idiot of yourself. Can't you see she's a cheap little pickup? Her behavior with Jim is disgraceful."

"Stop being so bitchy."

"Why shouldn't I be? You men are all alike. You see a pretty new face and try to think of a way to bed her down."

"Oh stop it, Ruth, will you?"

"Then what's your excuse for taking off today like that?"

"I think Kay is doing a good job. That's all that matters, as far as I'm concerned."

"So you have to take her on an all day outing to tell her that?"

"It wasn't an all day outing."

"How can an eye doctor be so blind? That little tramp is out to take you for all you're worth. Can't you see that?"

"You're making yourself sound ridiculous."

"Ridiculous, huh? Look what she did to Jim. He's devastated. She hasn't gone out with him for two nights. How she gloated that she could woo him away from his fiancée for a couple of one night stands and then drop him."

"Ruth, shut up."

"What?"

"Stop giving me that phony Sarah Heartburn bit. Jim worked late one night, then went to Petionville with the two O.D.s and tonight Kay was dining with me. If he's devastated about Kay, that's his problem."

"You'll pay for your fun and games, mark my words. You've already forgotten about the attaché case, haven't you—how she lied she didn't have it."

"I have it now and that's what's important, isn't it? At least nothing was taken from it."

"Next time maybe you'll remember to lock it. Your carelessness is going to get both of us in trouble. You're just lucky nothing was taken. You'd have plenty of explaining to do to U.S. Customs. But, Doctor, let's get to the point: what does that say about the character and intentions of your girl friend?"

Kay was stunned. She knew Mac had taken the attaché case. He had already admitted it to her, but listening to him make the admission to Ruth gave her a strange feeling inside. Would she ever be able to trust him? Even his kisses, she knew now, were not what they seemed.

"Will you stop that babbling, Ruth," Mac said, "and tell me, are you or aren't you coming to Port-au-Prince with me? Otherwise, I'll take someone else."

"You mean like Kay? Oh no, you don't. I'm coming with you."

Kay retreated from the hall and reentered her room. The conversation she overheard was depressing, especially after he put her through the emotional wringer he did today.

Did he care that every time he kissed her he triggered emotions in her that she couldn't ignore? He knew what he was doing to her.

If he did care, he would have told Ruth something else instead of inviting her to Port-au-Prince with him. Kay buried her face in her hands and wept silently. Perhaps she was only another pretty face to Mac, as Ruth intimated, and nothing else mattered.

But she cared, cared for him deeply. She knew that and had known it, even during the short period of time she had been in Haiti. Was that really so terrible? It was terrible if he was selling drugs or smuggling copycat glasses into the country. She wasn't thinking straight.

Yet, he had asked her out next week. If he was going to be in Port-au-Prince, she wondered if he would be back in time. Funny, that he hadn't told her he was going to be away. Why was he really taking Ruth to Port-au-Prince?

Chapter 6

"*Mademoiselle*, I'm sorry to have caused so much trouble."

Kay turned. Michel, the bellboy, was at the front desk and beckoned to her.

"What trouble?"

"I put Dr. MacDonald's attaché case in your closet."

"You don't have to apologize for that."

"I didn't know how valuable it was. I should have been more careful."

"Who told you it was valuable?"

"No one told me, but it was the way the doctor acted when he discovered what I had done."

"What did he say?"

"He was very upset."

"Don't worry about it, Michel."

"Did you return the case to him?"

"He has it, if that's what you mean."

"Again, *mademoiselle*, my regrets if I've caused you any distress."

"Really, don't mention it."

"Kay, I'm waiting for you in the jeep," Mac called to her, "across the street."

"If you'll excuse me, Michel," she said, "I have to go to work."

"I saw Michel speaking to you," Mac said, as Kay settled next to him. "What did he want?"

"Nothing."

"Sure was a long conversation about nothing." He smiled at her. "I have something more important to speak to you about." He reached out and clasped both of her hands in his. "I hope my conversation with Ruth at dinner last night didn't upset you."

"Why should it?" Kay said flippantly, but she avoided looking directly at him.

"I wouldn't want it to, for one thing." He released her hands and tilted her chin towards him. "I thought so," he said. She felt the tears prick her eyelids. At least he wasn't laughing at her. If only he would take her in his arms now and tell her he loved and needed her; tell the truth about that attaché case and the frames. She'd forgive him for everything. She squeezed her eyes shut and the tears spilled over her cheeks.

"Ruth and I have been good friends for a long time," he was saying, "and Ruth assumes more than she should frequently." He stepped on the accelerator and pulled away from the hotel.

The memory of Ruth's remarks still hurt. Of course, Mac was unaware she had overheard the later conversation.

"If you don't want her to, then why do you let her?" asked Kay.

"Well, it's hard. We've been through a lot together. She came to me after her divorce. She needed someone then desperately."

The word *needed* reverberated ominously. "You mean you were the first man to come along," Kay said bitterly.

"I tried to help her."

"She looks rather well adjusted to me."

"After some of the unfortunate experiences she has had with her ex, I can't make her life more miserable than it has been."

There wasn't much else to say, Kay thought. He apparently felt he had to protect Ruth.

"I'm going to discharge Nicole today and take her home after work. Would you like to come with me?"

"Yes, very much." She turned to look at him and caught his eye, but he averted his gaze as if embarrassed by what he saw. She knew her eyes were glistening from unshed tears.

"We'll leave about an hour before closing."

When they arrived at the clinic, Mac, accompanied by Kay, went back to see Nicole.

"She's a very lucky little girl," Mac said, shaking his head in amazement after he had examined her. "All the blood cleared and she'll be as good as new." He tapped Nicole playfully on her head.

"If she's all right," Kay asked, "do you think she could get dressed and out of bed?"

"She'll have to be kept quiet. We can't have her tearing up and down the hall."

"I'll be responsible for her," Kay said.

Dr. Mac was still reluctant, uncertain. "That means you're going to have to keep a close watch on her while you're working."

"I know."

Their eyes held. He looked at her with such tenderness that Kay blushed.

"I'll leave the decision then up to you," he said, walking away.

"Come on, Nicole, we're going to show everyone what a well-behaved young lady you are." Nicole stared at her in bewilderment, not comprehending. But when she saw Kay reach for her dress, the child jumped up and down excitedly. Dressed and combed, Nicole took Kay's hand and they walked over to Jean-Pierre.

"Meet my new assistant," Kay said to him. She plunked

Nicole down on a chair and gave her a felt tip pen and paper. Nicole cuddled her doll next to her while she happily drew pictures.

"What's your dolly's name?" Kay asked, forgetting Nicole didn't speak or understand English. The child looked up at her with adoration in her eyes, saying, "Kay-Kay."

Kay knelt down and hugged Nicole. "You little darling."

"Kay-Kay," Nicole said.

Kay laughed. "Nicole has one answer to any question I ask."

There were quite a few children who came to have their eyes examined. Without fail, they all stopped to chat with Nicole and admire her doll. Even Mac came out to joke about the honorary staff member.

At lunchtime, Kay and Jean-Pierre shared a table with Nicole and a portion of their sandwiches. The food remained untouched on her plate while Nicole chattered away with Jean-Pierre.

"Eat, Nicole," Kay said, pointing to the sandwich.

"Kay-Kay."

"Kay-Kay wants you to eat." Kay picked up the sandwich and touched Nicole's lips with it. Nicole turned her head and pushed the food away.

"Jean-Pierre, what's the matter? Doesn't she like it?"

"Just like a woman. All she wants to do is talk." He spoke to Nicole in Creole. The child crumpled, her eyes filling quickly with tears.

"Jean-Pierre, whatever did you say to her?"

"I told her to shush and eat her lunch."

"That's no way to speak to a child. Tell her again, but more gently."

"Oh, women," he said, rolling his eyes heavenward.

Jean-Pierre leaned over to Nicole and whispered in her ear. She smiled, took a bite of her sandwich, and with her mouth full of food pronounced her secret for happiness, "Kay-Kay."

When she was through eating, Nicole wandered back

into the clinic by herself while Kay gathered up the debris from the table. She was returning to her station when Ruth barreled towards her, one hand holding Nicole's.

"And who was the genius who let this kid loose?" Angrily, she gestured towards Kay. "I suppose this was your brilliant contribution to our health maintenance program."

"Yes, it was my idea," Kay stated calmly. "Nicole is being discharged today."

"Discharged patients don't have the run of the place, in case you didn't understand clinic procedure," she said. "When patients are discharged, they go home."

"But this is a child. She can't go home by herself," Kay said.

"Then she should stay in bed until it's time for her to leave."

"She's not bothering anyone, Ruth."

"How would you know? You're too busy making eyes at Jean-Pierre."

"How dare you! Jean-Pierre and I were coming in from lunch when you rushed down the hall with your complaints."

"Does Dr. Mac know that Nicole is out of bed?"

"Yes."

"Then you won't mind if I refresh his memory, will you?"

Five minutes later Ruth left Mac's cubicle, quite cowed, as she proceeded down the hall to her own post of duty, ignoring Kay completely.

About an hour before closing time, Mac told Kay to get ready to leave.

As soon as Nicole recognized the route, she became impatient, bouncing up and down on Kay's lap, singing a Creole song. The squeaky vocalizing made the ditty sound more like a nursery rime; but the child's joy at going home was unmistakable.

The jeep had barely pulled to a stop when Nicole flung open the door and ran home, crying, *"Maman, maman."* The older woman was in the yard preparing dinner over a charcoal pit. She heard the cry and came to meet her long lost daughter with arms outstretched.

Dr. Mac and Kay trailed behind as the mother yelled, "*Respe*," and waved them towards her, breaking with the usual tradition of waiting for "*Hono*" before welcoming visitors.

Mac assured the mother that Nicole was healed and she could stay home from now on. This was one translation Kay could figure out for herself. The sheer delight of the mother having her child next to her was a tableau Kay would long cherish.

Kay waved good-bye to Nicole, who stood near her mother, one hand clutching her mother's skirt.

"I feel like we've performed our good deed for the week," Kay said.

"Have dinner with me tonight and you'll be performing your second good deed for the week."

Kay felt so happy about reuniting Nicole with her mother that not even Ruth could upset her. "Where should we eat?" she asked. "At the hotel?"

"No, I don't think that would be wise."

Obviously, he wanted to avoid a repeat of last night's performance, Kay realized.

He thought for a minute. "Tell you what. I'll make some reservations. A special girl deserves to eat in a special place."

He pulled into his parking slot at the hotel. "Meet me in the lobby in about an hour. Give you enough time to get ready?"

Kay nodded.

This was one night she wanted to dress very carefully. She chose a ruffled and shirred top of crepe polyester in champagne with a midcalf skirting of black taffeta. To think that she hesitated packing this because she felt she'd never get a chance to wear it. She giggled in retrospect when she recalled how she had impulsively decided at the last minute to bring it. Tonight she was going to make use of it.

She brushed her hair till it shone like spun gold, clipped a pair of wafer thin domes to her ears, also in champagne. She opened the door to her room and gave it a fast inspection to see if she had forgotten anything.

Then she stepped out into the hall, closing the door softly, and glanced in the direction of the lobby. There he was, standing at the foot of the stairs, waiting for her.

What was there about a white dinner jacket that made a man look so exciting. This man, certainly. The broad shoulders, the face slightly tanned, the generous mouth. Her heart quickened. Who wouldn't find such a man charming.

He looked up at her when he heard the rustle of her skirt. He said not a word as he watched her descent, but the smile on his lips and in his eyes made Kay's heart leap a little more. He reached for her hand and her nerve endings tingled as he tucked it under his arm.

He held the door of the jeep open for her, then waited till she carefully gathered her skirt around her before gently closing the door.

Kay was so content to be sitting next to him that she indulged in a daydream they were on a road going nowhere. That was all she wanted out of life, to be near him.

"You haven't asked me where I'm taking you," Mac said. "Do you always go so willingly into strange men's cars?"

"No, of course not," she said, reddening, disconcerted lest he read her innermost thoughts. "But where are we going?"

"There's a magical place called Creme de la Creme between here and Cap Haitien. The specialty of the house is flaming rock lobster on a bed of rice and black dried mushrooms. Does that make your mouth water? It's one of my favorite places and I hope it will be yours, too."

The restaurant resembled a sprawling villa nestling in a garden of hibiscus, huge Shasta daisies and poinsettias surrounded by the regal stateliness of Royal palm trees. There were spotlights on the flowers, on the trees, and even aimed at the building itself, like the stage setting for a movie.

Inside was an extension of a Hollywood fantasy. The ambiance was Louis XV, expensive, seductive, muted. Banquettes, upholstered in pale blue, placed strategically in curved alcoves, enhanced the intimacy of dining.

The walls were decorated with panels of light blue quilted satin, alternated with silken like tapestries of flowers in pale rose.

Kay admired a nearby table setting. The crystal was Baccarat and the china, Sevres, engraved with the crest of the House of Bourbon.

Standing ready to pay homage to a French court of yore were the waiters, dressed as footmen from a bygone era.

"Like it?" Mac asked, observing Kay.

"It's fantastic."

The maître d' approached.

"Reservations for two for Dr. MacDonald," Mac said.

"It's Andre's table, Doctor?"

Mac nodded.

"Right this way." The maître d' beckoned to a waiter standing at the far end of the room.

"Good evening, Andre," Mac said.

"*Bon soir*, and what will it be this evening, Doctor, your usual?"

"Yes."

"And for the *mademoiselle*, the same?"

"Right."

"I'm assuming the usual is the specialty of the house," Kay said.

"Hope you don't mind," Mac said.

Kay shook her head.

What they talked about during dinner, Kay never could recall. She knew they had talked. All she could ever recall later was the thrill of being alive; and perfection, made even more beautiful by the food, the wine, and dining with this distinguished man.

Afterwards when they danced she was sensitive to his arms around her as he held her close.

"The food is excellent; but the dancing is better," he said, his lips brushing against her cheek. Kay's happiness knew no bounds. The unpleasant conversation she had overheard between Ruth and Mac receded into the background, having never existed.

The evening drew quickly to a close, too quickly for Kay. She felt like Cinderella; although she knew her coach wasn't going to turn into a pumpkin because it was a jeep. That was the only thing she was sure of.

"Why so quiet?" Mac asked, as they drove back to the hotel.

How could she tell him she was suddenly sad and withdrawn, like a bystander observing something she was certain was happening to someone else. She knew that events would never be the same, even if she and Mac were to return to the same place in the future. It was absolute sorcery, being in the company of an exciting male like Mac and then, transported by magic carpet to the Never Never Land of Creme de la Creme."

"Didn't you have a good time?" Mac asked shyly.

"I had a wonderful evening. I'm still under the spell."

He laughed. "I hate to be the first to break that spell, but unfortunately, I have to talk about a couple of mundane items."

Uneasy, she turned her head to study the silhouette of his profile. The past two days had been so uncomplicated, so simple, so wondrously lighthearted, that mentally she entreated him to spare her any disclaimer to the contrary. He kept his eyes on the road and grew serious.

"I'm going to be gone on Tuesday, Wednesday, Thursday, Friday, and Saturday because I have to be at the hospital in Port-au-Prince for cataract surgery. Think you can watch the store for me?" He turned his face to meet her gaze, the corners of his mouth quirking up in a grin.

"I thought you told me you didn't do any surgery since your malpractice suit."

"Is that what I told you?"

Kay nodded.

"I guess I'll have to be careful what I say in the future, won't I?" He chuckled. He took her hand and brought it to his lips. "You're really something, Kay."

She was disappointed he was lying to her. Why was he really going to Port-au-Prince? Who was he meeting there? What was Ruth's role in this?

"Aren't you going to wish me a successful trip?" he asked.

"Oh sure," she said indifferently.

"Before I forget," he said matter of factly, "that Haitian who had come in with the lid infection I treated the other day . . ."

"Monsieur Du Pont?"

"That's the one. He'll be returning for a fresh dressing on Tuesday, so when you go to work tomorrow, take his patient card over to one of the nurses. The nurses know he gets some glaucoma drops in the other eye and he's to get his usual dose, even though we're running short."

"Don't the drug companies contribute any of the medicine here?"

"They do. But we need more, that only dollars can buy."

"Why don't you hold a drive to raise money?"

"Kay, this is a clinic and I'm proud to be associated with it because whatever we've accomplished here has been achieved without the hard sell and hype of a PR agency. People see what we do and they contribute."

"But many more would be informed if you'd publicize the good work of the clinic."

"This is not a commercial enterprise," he replied testily.

"All the more reason why there would be many who would gladly and willingly donate funds."

"Look, Kay, I've been here at the clinic a little longer than you and I'm sensitive to its needs. You're still a novice."

"I may be a novice here, but as a model, I know what the right kind of publicity can do."

"I thought that was a part of your life you wanted to forget."

"I . . ."

"Wait a minute, why are we arguing?" He reached for her hand. "I'm sorry if I seem adamant but this is a blind spot with me. Let's talk about something more neutral, OK?"

"Is there any other procedure or patient I should know about?" she asked, hoping her additional question would jog his memory with the news she wanted him to disclose about Ruth.

"Nothing I can think of at the moment."

Nothing you can't think of or nothing you don't want to think of, thought Kay.

"You'll be busy, though, like we always are."

They pulled into the hotel parking lot and entered the lobby. Mac followed Kay up the stairs and stood behind her, his arms wrapped around her waist as she fumbled with the key.

He lifted the hair over her ear. "Am I making you nervous?" he whispered. He nipped the lobe of her ear. She giggled, then unlocked the door to her room.

"This beautiful evening deserves a beautiful beginning, not an ending," he said. Kay went to him gladly. Then his arms were around her. His kiss was gentle but insistent. She arched her body towards him as his mouth dropped down to her neck, leaving a trail of kisses wherever his lips touched.

Then he stopped suddenly, raising his head to look at her, his breath uneven. "I want you, Kay. I've always wanted you, from the first time I saw you."

Kay backed away, shaking her head. She didn't trust her emotions any longer.

"Don't run away. You want the same thing. I know you do." He reached for her again, encircling her and pulling her to him. "Come back to Boston with me. We'd make a great team, you and I."

A sharp knock on the door stopped them both, as if frozen in time. She clapped her hand over his. He placed a finger on her lips and mouthed, "Sh-h."

"Kay, are you in there?" Ruth's voice came across loud and shrill.

"I'll have to answer that," Kay said.

"Why?" he asked, kissing her.

"She knows I'm in here."

He shrugged his shoulders.

Kay smoothed out any telltale wrinkles in her dress, patted her hair in place, and tried to regain some semblance of composure. She waited until Mac ducked into the bathroom before she opened the door.

"And where have you been, all gussied up like that?" Ruth asked. "Sure took you awhile to get to the door. Have you seen Dr. Mac, by the way," she continued, not giving Kay a chance to reply.

"I'm right here," he said, emerging from the bathroom. "What is it?"

"I didn't see you at dinner and you didn't answer my rap on your door. I was worried that maybe you'd forgotten you have to be in Port-au-Prince tomorrow."

"No, I haven't forgotten about it," he said crisply.

"You haven't forgotten about a lot of things, I see," she said. Her dark eyes smoldered like live coals at Kay, who met that glare head on. "There are a couple of procedures I want to talk to you about."

"Can't it wait till morning?" Mac asked disgustedly.

"No, it can't. I might forget."

"All right, if you insist. I'll be seeing you, Kay," he said, winking at her, as he followed Ruth out of the room.

"You should be spending the night of our departure with me," Ruth chided, her strident speech echoing and reechoing through the hall.

"What are you trying to hand me?" Mac's voice was rough, harsh. "You know the procedures as well as you know your name."

The closing of a door ended the scenario, putting it out of earshot for Kay.

Kay listened and waited hopefully, expecting Mac to knock and return to her shortly. When he didn't, she got ready for bed, carefully hanging up the enchanted dress she wore for the evening. For a few hours tonight she had been in another world. How could it be otherwise than enchanted when she knew she was in love with Mac.

She had been aware of it for some time, but not until tonight did she dare believe the tug of her emotions. She thought he had the same feeling towards her, although he never said as much.

He had asked her to come to Boston. She was troubled. He never said he loved her, only wanted her.

There was no doubt that he and Ruth were lovers, perhaps still are. Their long acquaintanceship certainly pointed to that. Besides, there was no such thing as a platonic relationship between a man and a woman, she ought to know that,

She looked at her watch. Two hours had elapsed since Mac left her. While dreaming and thinking, she hadn't heard him return to his room. Then, as if an answer to her question, a door opened down the hall and she heard Mac's voice, "OK, Ruth, see you tomorrow bright and early. Get a good night's rest."

She heard his footsteps approach her door and stop. She wanted to jump up and yank it open and shoo him in, but no, if he wanted to see her, he must knock himself. The pause before her door was only momentary as she heard his footsteps move away and he proceeded down the stairs. Seconds later she heard a car start and leave the hotel parking lot. Where would he go at this hour of the night?

Kay sat down slowly on the bed, completely devastated. She couldn't believe it. She didn't want to believe it. He had been in Ruth's room ever since he left hers. How could he? She had a sick feeling in the pit of her stomach that only added to this newly discovered distress.

One minute he was making love to her and the next, he was with Ruth; probably because he didn't get what he wanted in here. She shook her head in disbelief. She had been a fool to think he would have any feeling for her. How could he be so insensitive? The evening had held so much promise for her; for both of them, she thought.

Stop and think. Were his advances a little too calculating, as if he were working from a script? Did the script include dinner at Creme de la Creme? She refused to presume that he took her out for her company alone. You never get anything for free, don't you know that by now, she reflected bitterly. Not even dinner. There is no such thing as a free lunch. Even Biff taught her that.

Ruth must have had a good laugh at her naivete. How could Mac betray her like that by staying in Ruth's room? How long did it take to review a couple of procedures, anyway? Certainly, not two hours.

Unconsciously, she clenched her fists until her nails dug into her palms. She tried to fight off the growing despair that engulfed her. How could he destroy the beautiful, loving time they had had together in an instant, so easily?

Even more important was the fact he would refute what he told her about surgery. That made her uneasy. He had stated firmly he didn't do any more, so why did he say he was going to Port-au-Prince to do cataract surgery? Was he going to meet someone there to get rid of that attaché case?

She shivered at the chill settling over her. Well, since she had once lied to him about that attaché case, this was the lie he owed her.

Chapter 7

"You're going to be working with me this week while Mac is gone," Jim said, as he and Kay rode to the clinic together the next morning.

He glanced up into his mirror. "Oh, oh."

"Jim?"

"Don't turn around, but I think we're being followed."

"Do you know who it is?"

"No, I've never seen him before. It's not a Haitian."

"What are we going to do?"

"We're pretty close to the clinic. Maybe if I speed up, I can lose him."

The rest of the way Jim held forth in a chatty monologue. She suspected he did it to keep her mind off their pursuer. But Kay wasn't listening. Instead, she let her own thoughts wander miles away, seventy-five miles away that is, in Port-au-Prince.

What was Mac doing at the moment? Is he really operating or is he using that as a ploy for something else? Where will he and Ruth stay? Together? In one room?

She was furious with herself for allowing any man to

reduce her to tears the way Mac had. Even now, thinking of him, she could feel the tears well up in her eyes. Thank goodness, she could lose herself in her work.

By the time Jim and Kay arrived at the clinic, the other car had vanished.

"The coast is clear," Jim announced. "You can relax. We lost him."

Despite such assurances, Kay swiveled her head towards the rear, searching for the unknown before leaving the car, then quickened her step towards the clinic.

"Kay, slow down. No one is following us," Jim called.

The first patient was already waiting at Jim's station when they entered. The ten-year-old boy was nearsighted and badly needed glasses. Jean-Pierre told Kay the boy's right ear had been partially ravaged by an ulcer. He had had glasses before, but couldn't wear them because the glasses kept falling off the lad's nose.

"See if one of the nurses has a piece of elastic," Kay said. Jean-Pierre looked at her, puzzled about the request. "I have an idea that might keep those glasses in place."

Kay tied the elastic from one temple of the frame to the other to wrap around the back of the child's head, firmly anchoring the glasses on his one ear. Once the glasses were in position, the boy's happiness was mirrored in his bobbing head, looking up and down, everywhere. He had suddenly discovered what his eyes could do for him.

"Look at that precious child," Kay said to Jim. "How thrilled he is that he can see."

"You have great sensitivity towards children, don't you?" Jim said.

"I like children, if that's what you mean."

"Anyone can like children, but you have a deeper feeling, empathy, or something. I've noticed it before."

"There's Jean-Pierre still speaking to that boy," Kay said, anxious to divert attention away from herself. "I hope he's all right."

Jim hailed Jean-Pierre. "Is there something wrong with the child?"

"Not at all. The boy stopped to tell me that everything everywhere looks new and so pretty with his glasses."

The boy wasn't the only one who discovered what sight could do. An older patient brought in her prayer book to test her vision after Kay fitted her with a pair of glasses. She felt her prayer book, not the official eye chart, was the ultimate gauge to measure the accuracy of the glasses.

Despite a busy schedule at the clinic, the days passed slowly for Kay. She wondered how she was going to get through the rest of the week. She had dinner the first night with Jim.

"Finish up, Kay," Jim said. "We're going dancing."

"Now? Tonight?"

"Why not?" Who could take that silly grin plastered all over his face seriously.

"We're going to go to the same place."

"Should I change my dress?"

"Hey, you look great just the way you are."

Although she had said yes to dancing again with Jim, she questioned whether her feet could endure another assault. The place was a little more crowded than before. How did Jim manage to get a reservation so fast? True, they weren't there for dinner, only drinks, but somehow, things weren't like they seemed.

"There's the music and a nice slow step, my specialty," Jim said, holding out his arms to Kay. She rose slowly, as if she were going to the guillotine. "I'm better now," he said, grinning at her hesitation.

As they danced Jim was busily scanning the dance floor. She watched his eyes as he found someone, recognized someone. His eyes narrowed. Whom did he see?

She looked in the same direction. Biff? What would he be doing here? No, it couldn't be. For a moment, the way that guy held his head, she could have sworn it was he.

Without warning, Jim pulled her close, whirling her towards the other end of the floor.

"Jim, stop that," she said, trying to push away.

"Don't resist me, Kay," he whispered in her ear, his cheek was on hers. "This is a matter of life and death. We're leaving this place shortly. Don't talk." His arm was around her waist, as he literally shoved her through the crowd to the car.

She watched the car pick up speed. "I hope you have a good excuse for your behavior, Mr. Barlow."

"I do."

"You're going too fast," Kay said. "Slow down or we'll both be killed. Jim, slow down. Did you hear me?"

"I heard you."

"What's the rush about, anyway, and this better be good."

"There's a very dangerous guy back there."

"Oh, really?"

"Too dangerous for a lovely girl like you."

"How many drinks did you have, Mr. Barlow, when I wasn't looking?"

"Only one, like you." He looked in his mirror. "I knew that was going to happen. We have a tail on us. I'm surprised he showed his face in a public place."

"But what does he want?" Kay asked.

"I have something he wants."

"Then give it to him."

"You don't know what you're saying so I'll forgive you. Listen to me carefully, Kay. I'll drop you off at the hotel and keep going. I think I can shake that guy."

"And if you can't?"

"I hope so, but I don't want you in the car if the party gets rough. Go to your room and wait for me. When I return, I'll knock on your door—two taps. Don't open the door to anyone else except me. Got it?"

After an hour had elapsed and Jim had not returned, Kay began to worry. Should she call the police? Maybe something happened to him. A car accident. The way he was driving was obscene.

Another hour passed. Why worry? Jim didn't really give a time period when he'd return. Then she heard the two light taps. When she opened the door, she wanted to throw her arms around him she was so relieved to see him, but he brushed her aside, saying, "In the future, I don't want anyone to see the two of us together. Dining together at the hotel is out also from now on." He finished speaking but then continued to stare at Kay as if she were a stranger.

"I think you know more than you're telling me. I had a heck of a time trying to shake that character tonight; and somehow I've got an idea he knows you. Kay, I want you to tell me the truth. What was the real reason you came to Haiti?"

She felt her anger begin to surface. If he weren't her best friend's fiancé, she'd tell him to shove it. Instead, she asked meekly, "Sir, can I use my driver's license for I.D.?"

He glared at her. "You think this is a joke, don't you?"

"I came because I wanted to help the Haitians."

"I don't believe you, but I'll overlook that. Who was the guy who told you about this operation?"

"The school told me about the eye clinic." Two can play this game as easily as one, she thought.

"You're not listening to me. You won't admit it because you don't want to or because you don't know?"

"Let's leave it at that," said Kay.

"I thought that by this time I could trust you and you could trust me. It seems I was wrong."

"Think what you want."

"How do I know I can trust you?"

"You'll just have to take me at face value. What you see is what you get, Mister."

"Have it your own way. I'll warn you, Kay, you'll find that the guy at the head of this operation can be quite insistent, with no exceptions, about confessions."

"I think you better leave, Jim."

"I'll leave on one condition. Tell me who sent you?"

"I told you, the school."

"What were you offered in return . . . something to sweeten the pot?"

"I volunteered for this. The school sent me because I volunteered."

"There were other graduates, weren't there?"

"So what's the point?"

"But only you were selected from your school."

"How should I know?"

"That's your story and you're stuck with it. How can I find out if I can trust you when you won't even give me honest answers?"

"I don't have to sit here and listen to this garbage." She walked over to the door and opened it. "Get out."

"I want you to tell me the name of the man who sent you down here." He remained seated.

Then her anger exploded. Why was she left in the lurch? She didn't know whom to contact even if she found any evidence. She was in a very dangerous position. She should never have consented to getting involved with Tripwire. And where in hell is the agent? It's apparent it's not Jim.

Jim sat on the edge of his chair, one foot forward, ready to pounce on anything she'd say. Finally, he rose and shook his head. "Have it your own way. Sure hope you don't get hurt in this."

"I told you to leave," Kay said.

Later, Kay reflected on her scene with Jim. Too bad Mary Ellen wasn't privy to this conversation. Kay almost pitied her. Did she know what she was getting into, marrying Jim? Kay shook her head in bewilderment.

She doubted Jim's veracity. Were they really followed by another car? There was traffic on the road. Maybe Jim had a rendezvous to keep. Took him two hours to return. Those two hours could have been spent in a meeting.

At first she thought Jim would be the most dependable

person at the clinic, someone that she could count on and lean on if she ever needed help or rescue. Not any more.

The rest of the week she had quiet dinners by herself. Truthfully, it was a relief not to be given the third degree. She missed Mac. She missed seeing him during the day; just the way he'd scrutinize her when she handed him a chart. Ironic that she didn't come to Haiti looking for romance; yet romance sought her. It took his absence to make her realize the void he left in her life, despite everything.

When Friday at last rolled around, Kay was grateful that the weekend would soon commence. She looked forward to Saturday as a day to get away by herself, away from the clinic.

"Got any big plans for tomorrow?" Jim asked at lunch, as he sat down opposite her.

"Are you sure that it's safe to be seen together?" She was suspicious of the phony friendliness.

He laughed. "Don't be so literal."

"Isn't that how I'm supposed to be?"

"You didn't answer my question, as usual," Jim said.

"I don't have to."

"Seems like I heard that before. I thought you might be doing some sight-seeing. No cross examination. Only an innocent curiosity."

"The management thanks you on that. I'm planning to go to the Iron Market in Port-au-Prince."

"Good. Now that's something I'm an expert on."

"Suppose I don't want your help," Kay said, annoyed with this new domineering Jim.

"Whether you like it or not, you're going to get it."

"I'm sure I'll have no trouble finding my way to the Iron Market."

"I wouldn't want anything to happen to you."

"How touching. But I'm getting a little fed up with your condescension. I didn't ask for your help. I don't need it and I don't want it,"

"Now you listen to me, Kay, before you do something foolish and get yourself shot at."

She stared at him. She never expected Jim to talk to her like that.

"I'm going to draw a map for you so you won't get lost, and I'm going to let you use my car, too."

"Thought there was a bus I could take."

"Wouldn't hear of it," he said. "Besides, if you have the car, you can return when you wish. You do have an international driver's license, don't you?"

"That was the first thing I was told to get before coming to Haiti."

"Good enough."

She watched him walk back to the clinic. She mused over his volatile personality. Working with him, he was just the nicest guy: kind, understanding, and solicitous of her and the patients. But once away from the clinic he became insolent and overbearing. How Mary Ellen ever got herself hooked up with someone like this was beyond her.

At dinner that night at the hotel, while Kay was finishing up her dessert, she was again joined by Jim.

"It's all right, it's all right," he said, sitting next to her. He showed her the map he had drawn. "I'd like to go over this with you."

"That won't be necessary. I can read it as well as you."

"You're going to get my help, Kay Thompson, whether you like it or not. All through with dinner? March right up to your room.

"And suppose I want to have a second cup of coffee?"

"Kay, be reasonable."

"Look who's talking about being reasonable."

"Kay, I have something important to show you on the map."

"Unless this is a treasure map, I'm not really interested. Now you listen to me, James. You drew a map for me. That's fine. The rest of the way, I'm on my own. You have pushed me too far, Mr. Barlow, and I refuse to jump any more."

"I guess I came on kind of strong, didn't I? I apologize. Tell me, when are you planning to return to your room?"

"When I get good and ready." Kay continued to sip her coffee slowly as she watched other diners and ignored Jim.

"The Iron Market is a very colorful place."

"Do tell."

"I said I was sorry."

"You'll have to do a lot better than that," Kay said, leaving the table, with Jim following closely behind.

When she opened the door to her room, he entered quickly. "Let's get this over with," she said.

He placed the map on her desk, pointing as he spoke, "The market is near the International Exposition Grounds. I marked it on the map for you, here. Between President Truman Boulevard and the waterfront are the exposition grounds and east of the Expo is the Iron Market."

"I'm sure I'll find it."

"Prices are lower there than in any of the shops."

"And why couldn't you give me this information downstairs in the dining room? Too classified, perhaps?"

"There's one more thing," Jim said, placing a finger against his lips. "Do you have a piece of paper?"

"Enough with the melodrama, already. There's no one in this room except the two of us."

He shook his head gravely.

Kay shrugged her shoulders and gave him a sheet of hotel stationery. Her eyes widened as she watched him write one word: Tripwire. She couldn't believe it. After all this time? What had kept him so long from telling her? Could she trust him at this late date?

Jim watched her reaction. "You don't believe me, do you?"

"How can I?" Kay asked. "We've seen each other daily, had dinner and lunch together, even gone out dancing, and not a word from you. Were you testing me or what?"

Jim laughed. "No, I just got the word."

Determined to trip him, Kay asked, "From whom?"

"How does the name of Willoughby sound to you?"

"All right, but why did it take so long?"

"Mr. Willoughby had been suddenly taken ill and turned the communique over to another staffer and I guess it was shuffled with some other papers on his desk. But why worry about that now? We can work together at last as a team."

"Comes the day when you work with me as a team."

"Kay, I know you're a little upset with me."

"A little? The understatement of the year."

"Well, a lot."

"Let's get something straight right now. If you think I'm going to be a stooge for some half-baked plan you've cooked up, brother, you have another guess coming."

"Kay, this is serious business."

"And what else is new?"

"Can I depend on you?"

"Depends on what you want me to do."

"Didn't Willoughby talk to you about your role?"

"He indicated that my involvement included keeping my eyes open for the fakes and then contacting Tripwire."

"What are you uptight about, Kay? I'm Tripwire. That's all I want you to do. When you get to the Iron Market, be on the lookout for copycat glasses."

"And if I find something?"

"Call me. I'll do the rest. Last year I was in Brazil, working at an eye clinic something like ours, and with the help of another investigator, we launched a very successful sting operation."

"Have you checked out everyone at the clinic?"

"Yes."

"The nurses, optometrists, and Mac?" She was determined to get the truth about him. She was positive Jim would know, but her voice trembled when she asked.

Jim looked at her sharply. "Everyone, but why Mac?"

"He had picked me up at the airport just at the moment my suitcase and an attache case were stolen by a guy on a bike."

"Yeah. I heard about that. That thief has been doing that for years, but Mac recovered them, didn't he?"

"Oh sure. He also admitted that the attaché case was his."

"So?" Jim asked dryly.

"But that's not the end. When we arrived at the hotel, Mac apparently had left his room key at the clinic and asked Michel, the new busboy, to place the case in the closet of his room. But Michel put the case in my closet by mistake."

"Why would he do that?"

"I had left my door unlocked that evening."

"For a good reason, I hope."

"I had just stepped out to post some letters in the mail drop downstairs."

"And you didn't see Michel?"

"I then decided on the spur of the moment to wander through the garden in the back."

"That makes sense, especially, at night."

Kay glared at him. She didn't like the change in Jim, either as an investigator or a friend. "Well, that's the truth. Michel must have dumped the case then in my closet."

"So why didn't you return it to Mac in the first place?"

"I was frightened."

"Of what?"

"It was intuitive. I had opened the case and found copycat designer frames, along with Ray-Ban sunglasses. Anyway, when Mac asked me if I had seen the case, I lied and said no."

"That was stupid. So far I fail to understand why you think Mac's behavior is suspicious."

"That first night when you and I had gone out—when we returned, I checked the closet and the attaché case was gone."

"So that was the missing item that devastated you," Jim said.

"Since only Mac and Michel knew it was there," Kay continued, "I was convinced that Mac had entered my room and taken it."

"If anything, your behavior was more suspicious than Mac's."

"Why are you laughing at me? Don't you believe me?"

"Oh, I believe you, all right. You're just not a very good detective. What you don't know, Kay, is that U.S. Customs has been giving Mac these kits so he can recognize and familiarize himself with the fake frame from the genuine and the same for the Ray-Ban, if he should come across them here or even when he returns to the States."

"Why did Mac take that attaché case from my closet?"

"Really, Kay, the case belonged to him, anyway."

"And why did he tell me he was going to perform cataract surgery in Port-au-Prince when he had told me earlier that since his malpractice suit, he doesn't do surgery any more?"

"Is that what he said?"

"You didn't answer my question."

Jim grew silent, as if he were weighing each word. "I don't have an answer to that question. I'm sure Mac has, though. He is just too ethical a man to become involved in anything that is not honest. For awhile there, I thought you two were a couple."

"Whatever gave you that idea?"

"A lot of things," said Jim, ogling her. "But if you suspect him, that doesn't say much for your relationship, does it?"

She didn't want to tell him that his opinion of Mac was what she wanted to hear.

"Back to your trip tomorrow to the Iron Market. Do you know what to do now if you find anything?"

"But how can I detain anyone?"

"Call me. Stay where you are. I'll come out as soon as I can."

. . . .

The next morning, armed with her map, Kay left. That's when she realized she should have taken the bus. She had forgotten about her trip on this road the day she had arrived, in the first flush of excitement of setting out alone to the Iron Market.

Was it only ten days ago? So many things had happened: her relationship with Mac, and then Jim's I.D. as Tripwire. Still hard to digest. But he knew Willoughby and he knew the password. Have to accept him for what he is. She was going to go to the Iron Market and have fun; that is, if she ever got there in one piece.

She hugged the road jealously. Her hands felt clammy; the steering wheel was already damp with perspiration. She kept her eyes focused in front of her, not once daring to let them wander over the side and the bottomless abyss she knew lay beyond her immediate vision.

The downhill grade increased the momentum of the car as it followed the snaked route around mountains that seemed to crowd her mercilessly. Kay put the car into Ll, hoping to slow her speed. Nothing happened. She tried L2, but the drag here didn't curb her pace. Frantically, she pumped the brake.

Just when she felt she had survived one road crisis, another menace appeared, barreling behind her, fast and furious. Kay looked in the rear mirror. The driver, whoever he was, was gesticulating wildly; first as if he were waving at her, then pointing straight ahead.

She didn't know what he wanted. But she couldn't stop here. She turned off onto Harbor Street and drove through a rundown hill district where tiny houses were packed together so close they appeared to be propping each other up.

That character was still pushing her. Suddenly he was alongside her. "Pull over to the curb."

Who in blazes did he think he was! He moved ahead of her, parked, and got out of his car.

She froze. There was no mistaking that sun bleached

hair and handsome devil-may-care face for anyone except Biff.

"Where did you come from?" asked Kay.

"The Eye Clinic."

"The Clinic? What were you doing there?"

"Looking for you."

"I don't believe you."

"Don't then, my Mary Contrary."

"I'm not your Mary Contrary."

"Why are you surprised to see me? Didn't you get my notes?"

"What notes?"

"I've got your number and this is no place for you."

Kay shrank away from him. "You scared the hell out of me."

"You walked out on me in the middle of a job."

"You deserved it."

"I won't belabor that point. But I need you, Kay, right now."

"I'm not interested in your tale of woe. How did you know I was here anyway?"

"I called your uncle, since I needed a model, and he told me. I have a very legitimate assignment to publicize the work being done at the clinic."

"I don't believe you."

"Here—take a look at the letter which gives me the authority to photograph the clinic, patients, and so on, for a booklet to be published by Clinics, International."

He waited for her to finish reading the letter. "I want you to be the model."

"Oh no, you don't."

"You owe me one, Babe."

"What are you talking about—after you had me blackballed so I couldn't get another job?"

"Let's let bygones be bygones. I want a favor from you."

"When didn't you ever?"

"Your clinic needs money for more medicines, facilities. The volunteer organization behind it hired me to publicize the good work the clinic is doing in the field. This is all for the benefit of the Eye Clinic. Even if you don't want to do me a favor personally, you wouldn't want to let the clinic down, would you?"

"No."

"Good girl. Can I stop by tomorrow for some pictures? I've got an idea on how I'd like you posed, in several heart stopping scenes in surgery."

"I'm not a nurse, Biff. I can't do that. Besides, there isn't any surgery performed there."

"We'll talk about it tomorrow then." He got back in his car and drove away.

She hated the idea of working with him again, but . . . maybe a couple of pictures would get him out of her life once and for all.

Kay turned her attention to the map Jim had drawn. This area where she was, was marked as Bel Air. She proceeded onto the waterfront with its crowded wharves and cargo boats.

She spotted the two Moroccan minarets first. Afterwards, it wasn't hard to find the two iron warehouses linked by a gate with the slender towers.

She parked the car on an off street and walked towards the Iron Market. Inside the gate were hundreds of stalls and thatched roof booths where vendors displayed their wares. Some sellers even sat on the ground with their wares spread before them on burlap bags. No copycat glasses in sight.

Kay wanted to look at everything before deciding what to buy. There were figurines sculpted from mahogany, handwoven sisal hats, sandals, tote bags, and necklaces made of poinciana seeds. There were hand-dyed rugs, Haitian primitives, and embroidered blouses. The shouts of hawkers as they threaded their way through the crowded aisles, their hampers crammed full of produce, added to the frenetic activity of the Iron Market.

Kay found some good carved wood items and paintings

buried amid chickens and vegetables. She selected an ashtray souvenir in the claw shape of Haiti for her uncle.

Then she saw the Haitian primitive she wanted to buy. Three Haitian women, dressed in red, purple, and yellow, walking with stately grace towards a market stall, carrying baskets of papayas, coconuts, and bananas on their heads.

She began to bargain with the seller about the picture. She had been encouraged when the vendor had greeted her in French. His price was high, higher than she wanted to pay, though, and she told him so.

"This print is very, very rare, *mademoiselle*," the vendor explained.

"What makes it so rare?" Kay asked.

"It's the last picture the artist painted before he died. You really like this print, don't you?"

"Yes, I do," Kay said, "but it's still too expensive for me."

"*Mademoiselle*," he said, spreading his hands in a nonchalant gesture, "this is not only the last picture the artist painted, but the only one in existence."

"Did you know the artist?" Kay asked.

"You might say that."

Kay stood there, staring at the print. It was colorful and typical of Haiti. She would have cared less if it were a reproduction or a copy of an original, she liked it and wanted it. Jim would probably tell her that was the wrong approach.

But if she paid the price asked, her budget for spending would be depleted. She didn't know what to do. Kay was sure, too, that since she looked like a tourist, his was a calculated attempt to see how much he could charge her and get away with it. She stood there, mulling over a decision, when without warning, someone seized her hand.

She recoiled.

"Need some help?"

She grabbed his arm joyously. "Oh, Mac, I'm so glad to see you."

He smiled at her enthusiastic greeting.

"I guess I'm an amateur when it comes to the art of haggling; but the vendor wants more than I can afford, and I . . ."

"How much is he asking?" he interrupted her.

Kay told him.

"That's a rip-off. Besides, that painting isn't even worth one gourd, let alone fifty."

"What do you know about Haitian primitives?" Kay asked.

"More than you do."

Kay stared at him in disbelief. Was this the man she missed all week, ached for, pined away for? She was also aware of the vendor gaping at them.

"Anyway, that's not what you're looking for, nor is it what you want."

Kay began to do a slow burn. "How do you know what I want?"

"You'd be surprised if I told you."

"But . . ." Kay started to say.

"Don't argue with me. I know where you can get the same print but a lot cheaper." Roughly, he jerked her arm away from the stall and pushed her towards the opposite side of the aisle.

What was with this guy—that he feels he always has to take charge of her life. He and his damned chauvinism.

"*Monsieur, mademoiselle,*" the vendor yelled. "Wait."

"I knew we'd get him to scream uncle," Mac muttered in Kay's ear.

"If the *mademoiselle* wants the picture for the price she had first said, I'll be happy to settle for that."

Kay took out her wallet.

Mac stopped her. "My treat. Something special we shared at a time when you needed me. It took me awhile myself to learn and perfect the technique of dickering or haggling or whatever you want to call it." The prize in his hand, he steered her toward the exit.

"I almost believed your hassling me was for real back there," Kay said.

"You're going to have to learn when to take me seriously," he said, "and when not to. The first rule you should know about being a successful bargainer is that you've got to let the seller know if he doesn't meet your final offer, you're going to walk out of his store. During the course of this scenario, you also inform him that what you want to buy is not worth the price he's asking and you know where you can get it cheaper."

"He also told me this was a rare print and the only copy."

"Wow. He pulled out all the stops. Talk about hard sell."

"Is all that part of the haggling game?" Kay asked.

"It amounts to bluffing and who can be the first to get away with the most outrageous offer and counteroffer."

"I'm glad you came along when you did."

"Only glad?" he asked.

"Happy. I thought you'd be busy at the hospital this time of the day."

"Do you really think I spend all day in surgery?"

"Well, I . . ." *Ask him if he had actually been operating.* "Never mind." She didn't like the sound of that. It emphasized her own insecure position with him.

"What are you so grim about, Kay? I came to the Iron Market because I had hoped to buy a souvenir for someone special."

"Let's go back then," she said uncertainly. "You didn't get a chance to make your purchase."

"I already did or didn't you notice? I see you've bought something else—that ash tray. Is that for the ogre in your life?"

"My uncle."

"What time did your bus arrive?" Mac asked.

"I didn't take the bus. Jim let me use his car."

"I see. I suppose you and he have been dining together."

"Sure. Why not?"

A sudden chill came between them. Kay was not immune to it. His eyes darkened. "Nothing," he said. "It's nothing. Everything OK at the clinic?"

"Yes."

"No problems?"

"Busy, unless you'd call that a problem. And how did your work go?"

"Fairly successful," he replied.

It wasn't surgery, she knew that. How could she ever believe him when he kept shelling out story after story?

"Say," he said, "I've got an idea. Ruth is going to stay on and monitor a couple of patients for me."

What patients? Something else was going on. She wished she knew what it was.

"Maybe Ruth could return in the jeep and I'll go back in Jim's car with you."

Kay couldn't help but breathe a sigh of relief. "It's nice to be wanted," he said, smiling at her reaction.

"I had forgotten how miserable that road is until I was on it," Kay said.

"Is that the only reason you want me to drive?" Their eyes held momentarily. Then Kay's vision drifted back to the Iron Market.

"Which reminds me. I better call Ruth and let her know my change of plans. Wait for me here. I'll be right back."

Kay watched the endless stream of pushcart vendors and country people carrying bundles of produce on their heads as they traipsed towards the Iron Market. She ought to be angry with him. What was the use of making such a resolute declaration? It was a delusion when he looked at her the way he did.

"It's all settled." Mac came up to her and seemed as pleased with himself as a schoolboy completing an onerous assignment. "Let's eat first and I'll give you a Cook's tour of the Expo grounds."

They lunched at one of the many sidewalk cafés on the landscaped plaza.

"This," Mac said, spreading his hands before him, "is

the tourist center of Port-au-Prince with its shops, theater, government buildings."

Kay let her eyes sweep briefly over the collection of boutiques, stores, cafes, and restaurants fronting on the square.

A vendor, who reminded her of a neighborhood ice cream seller peddling his products, had established himself smack dab in the middle of the plaza, extolling the virtues of the syrupy crushed ice in his wagon for anyone who cared to listen or to buy.

She looked but did not see because she was listening to the voice of the man she loved, watching his mouth and meeting the gaze of those blue gray eyes.

The two of them spent another hour or so walking up and down the plaza, his arm linked in hers, browsing in the shops.

The trip back to the hotel was extraordinarily uneventful. Though there was a constant flow of traffic, it was thinned out so as not to cause any undue congestion. Kay leaned back in her seat and relaxed.

"What have you been doing with yourself since I've been away?" Mac asked unexpectedly.

"Working, like you," Kay said.

"But you didn't work 24 hours a day, did you?"

Kay giggled. "I took time out for eating and sleeping."

"Did you go out anywhere?"

"Where would I go?"

"Oh, you know, dancing and nightclubbing."

"No."

"Not even with Jim?"

"Jim was working, too."

"Yeah, I know, another workaholic. Did you miss me?"

"Of course I did."

"That's what I want to hear."

Did he miss her? That's what she would have liked to ask him, but she was afraid that his reply would not be the one she wanted to hear.

Mac dropped her off at the hotel. "I want to check on something at the clinic. Be ready to leave for the Citadelle at 8:00 in the morning. Did you bring extra jeans with you?" Kay nodded. "Wear a pair tomorrow. We'll be on horseback."

She looked forward to Sunday, but she was disappointed that he didn't suggest they have dinner together this evening. At least, he wasn't dining with Ruth. That, she knew. Certainly, he wouldn't drive all the way back to Port-au-Prince to eat with Ruth, or would he?

She returned to her room and picked up the Haitian primitive she had acquired, smiling in retrospect of a wonderful day over a wonderful souvenir. She placed the picture at the far end of the room, then stepped back to admire and reexamine it.

The artist had truly captured the color, the brightness, the buoyancy of the people. She liked it. It had caught the flavor of the country.

She pursed her lips when she recalled Mac's words as he paid for it: to mark a special time when she needed him. Yes, she needed him, but he had never voiced a need for her. Doubts festered into uncertainty. Why? Why was it so difficult for him to reveal his true feelings to her? Afraid he might become vulnerable?

She selected a pair of beige jeans and a brown and white checked poplin blouse for tomorrow.

When she was in his arms she couldn't think and didn't want to. Sure, she was guilty of jumping to snap decisions in the past, purely on impulse. Not this time.

The gray area that remained was whether he's actually removing cataracts in Port-au-Prince. That could easily be a coverup for a smuggling operation.

Even Jim had no answers to this; especially, since Mac admitted to her the sole solution to the high cost of malpractice insurance rates was to quit surgery.

Perhaps by spending the day with him tomorrow, she could coax an explanation from him.

There was a light tapping at her door.

"You didn't think I'd let you go to sleep without saying goodnight, did you?" Mac asked.

He reached for her hands and wound them around his waist. He slipped his hand underneath her hair to the nape of her neck, bringing her close to him. "Aren't you glad I came in to tuck you into bed?"

Kay laughed. "Do you offer this service to all of your volunteers?"

He lowered his head to meet her lips with his. As the kiss deepened, Kay was bewitched. "Does that answer the question?" he asked. Enveloped in such an aura of contentment, she could forgive him for any slight she had endured in the past.

"Come to Boston with me, Kay. Together, the two of us will set the world on fire."

This wasn't a marriage proposal, only a statement of desire. It's not that he needed her or loved her, she reflected ruefully, only wants her.

He sat down on the edge of the bed, pressing her down to him. He kissed her gently then pulled her into a close embrace, burying his face in her hair.

He leaned away from her with his hands gripping her wrists. She dared not move. Her heart was hammering so loud it nearly deafened her.

He looked at her. His eyes had softened, but what Kay saw made her own heart burst. The tenderness, the love on Mac's face were all there, more than she had ever dreamed or imagined.

His lips closed hungrily on hers. Now Kay knew that not only desire but love as well was his, though he didn't say it. He didn't have to.

"Put your arms around me, Kay," he whispered in her ear. "Hold me." His lips met hers once again. The kiss was almost chaste, yet it stirred her senses to the very power of endurance.

She wrapped her arms tightly around him and wanted

to cling to him like this forever. She forgot the past, present and future. Now nothing was important except the two of them.

He reached out and touched her face. "Come to Boston with me," he said. She started to speak, but he placed a finger on her lips. "Don't say anything now, just return with me. I never want to let you go."

His lips brushed like a breath of air across her eyelids then closed on her mouth with a soft but insistent pressure.

There was a clatter of footsteps up the stairs, followed by a rapping on a door down the hall. "Dr. MacDonald, Dr. MacDonald, are you in there?"

"Maybe it's an emergency," Kay said.

"What kind of an emergency did you have in mind?" His fingertips lightly traced the outline of her mouth and trailed down her neck.

"I mean an eye emergency."

"Really?" He smiled. "Should I let you in on a secret? There aren't any eye emergencies unless there's an accident or some such."

"Maybe it is an accident."

"At this hour? I doubt it. Everyone's sleeping."

"Mac."

"Sh-h, don't say a word."

His mouth dropped to her neck. She opened her eyes and saw him watching her, attentive, expectant. A suggestive smile crossed his face.

As if on signal, more loud rapping was heard in the hall.

"Mac, listen."

"Don't pay attention to that. Pay attention to me."

"But, Mac, wait a minute, someone is looking for you and it may be serious."

A door opened. "I don't think the doctor is in. He must have gone out."

"That was Jim's voice," Kay said.

"You see, even Jim doesn't think I'm around. Only you and I know I'm here."

"Mac..."

"You don't really want me to go now, do you?"

"No."

"I didn't think so."

"But..."

"But what?"

"Suppose they begin looking for you, whatever the problem is, and find you in here with me?"

"So? I'm old enough for this, aren't you?"

"How will it look?"

"Are appearances that important to you?"

"Aren't they to you?"

"It all depends on the eye of the beholder and what I see now I want. Should I stick my head out of the door and tell them Jim said I wasn't here?"

"You're a devil," Kay said, laughing.

The footsteps withdrew downstairs and the hubbub subsided. Minutes later, the voices were back in the hall. A man was saying, "I don't know where he is. He doesn't answer his door."

"He's talking about you," Kay whispered.

"Sh-h, don't say a word," Mac said.

"What are we going to do," a second voice asked. "How could the Doc disappear without anyone knowing where he was."

"They're still looking for you," Kay said. "I hate to see you go. But it must be important, Mac, otherwise, they would have given up looking for you a long time ago."

"How do you know it's so important anyway?"

"Even if it's not life threatening, there is some kind of a problem, since they're still searching for you. Besides, you are in charge of the volunteer program and if you don't show, people might think something serious might have happened to you."

"It did. I fell for you."

"Mac, I think you better go."

"Now I'll need a good excuse to account for my absence. Got any ideas?"

"I hadn't thought about that."

"I can't tell them I was in here."

"No."

"And I can't tell them I was in my room, since they knocked on the door and I didn't answer."

"So where were you?"

"I was on my way to the clinic from where?"

"Mac, there's no one in the hall. You could beat a hasty retreat right now and no one would know the difference."

"Do you think so."

"Of course I do. Besides, whoever has been looking for you will be back and you'll have to go out and meet them eventually."

"I suppose you're right," he said at last, weighing what she had said. "Never argue with a woman." He leaned over one last time to press his lips on hers. "I'll see you later."

Kay watched him put his ear to the door and steal out into the hall.

How could anyone not love such a man? Tomorrow on the way to Milot, she was going to give him the answer she knew he was waiting for. She would return to Boston with him.

What a really glorious weekend it has been! Kay never felt so happy, so complete, so loving. Mac was everything and more that a girl could want. When she was in his arms, she couldn't think and didn't want to. Happily, she got ready for bed and looked forward to a day she knew would be the brightest in her life.

Chapter 8

The doorknob jiggled. Not again. Whoever those guys are, they're going to have to play cards somewhere else. In a spurt of anger, Kay yanked open the door.

"Oh no."

Biff stood there, a finger over his lips. "Oh yes," he whispered.

"What are you doing here?" she demanded.

"That's a fine way to greet a hard working guy so early in the morning," he said, pushing her back into the room. "You didn't forget about our date for today, did you?"

"I did, but I also forgot I have a date today."

"Tough."

"Couldn't we make it for another time?"

"Nope. I have to leave for Chicago in a couple of days. This won't take long, maybe an hour."

Kay stood there, uncertain. "Move, Kay. You'll have to get out of those jeans. Don't you have a nurse's uniform?"

"I told you I'm not a nurse."

"Wear whatever you wear then, when you report to the clinic. I'll wait for you downstairs."

Kay changed into her regular uniform and hurried into the dining room, hoping to find Mac. He wasn't around. She raced back upstairs and knocked on his door. No answer. She couldn't hear a sound coming from within. Why isn't he in his room getting ready? Where could he have gone? Back downstairs, she stopped at the desk and told the clerk to tell Mac she'd return in an hour.

As Kay and Biff pulled away from the hotel, Kay caught a glimpse of Mac with one of the maintenance men approaching the front of the hotel from the garden. To think she missed him within the space of a few seconds! She was silent on the way to the clinic.

"Don't you have anything to say to your good old buddy after all these years of absence?" Biff asked.

"No."

"Not even a how-have-you-been?"

"Let's get this over with already, if you don't mind."

"What are you so uppity about?"

"You can park over to the side," Kay instructed, as they neared the clinic.

"I'd like to get a shot of you at the entrance," Biff said, "so you run on ahead and I'll get my tripod and camera set up."

Kay stood to the side of the door, squinting at the camera.

"If you want these pictures to look good, start smiling." Biff adjusted his tripod. "Have you forgotten everything I taught you, love?" Biff yelled at her. "Don't look so glum, Kay."

She started to smile, then saw Mac's car. She felt sick, although what she was doing was nothing to be ashamed of. She knew how he felt about publicity for the clinic.

"Kay, wake up, smile. Not too much, just a little." Biff had cupped his hands over his mouth.

Mac walked up to the door. "Good morning," he said, looking right through her. She knew then he wouldn't understand. The voice was icy, the eyes, glacial. "Are you here for work or play?" he asked.

"It's my day off."

"I'm glad you told me. I wouldn't have known. Since you're in uniform, you might as well get a chart for me. I've got an emergency foreign body to remove."

She turned briefly to follow him into the clinic.

"Hold it, Kay. Fine," Biff called.

"Never mind," Mac said. "I'll get it myself."

"Another one just like that," Biff directed. "As if you're going to walk through the door. Turn your head a little to the right. Perfect."

Biff picked up his tripod and gadget bag and followed her into the clinic.

There was a cluster of Haitians standing in line, waiting to see one of the optometrists.

"I'd like to get some inside shots, Kay," Biff said. "Can you stand near this group so that it looks like you're attending them? Good. Now look cheerful. You're still the greatest model, kid. You give a uniform class, baby." He looked up from his focusing, a big grin on his face. "You sure haven't lost that spark, even in an out of the way place like Haiti."

For a moment, Kay's vision shifted. Mac stood there, observing her and listening. His face was impassive.

"Do you have any hospital patients here at all?" Biff asked, oblivious of Mac's presence. "I'd like to go for the dramatic shot, like maybe an I.V. bottle giving sustenance to an emergency case."

"We don't have anything like that," Kay said, "but there's a patient who was hit in the eye and he's confined to bed."

"Straight from Hollywood Casting. What more could I ask? Lead the way, my love. These pictures are going to play in Peoria and sell in Iowa."

"Just a minute, you two." Kay stopped. Her blood ran cold. "Who gave you the right to photograph the clinic anyway, Mr. . . . . uh?"

"My friends call me Biff. I have a letter from Clinics, International for this assignment. Here, read it for yourself," he said, handing the letter over to Mac.

Mac examined the letter and frowned. "Miss Thompson knows how strongly I feel about this issue."

"What issue?"

"Unwarranted publicity."

"You gotta be kidding, man. Clinics, International will be publishing a brochure about the clinic to cap a drive for money for medicine and supplies needed here. It's all in there," Biff said, pointing to the letter.

"I can read it as well as you," was the surly reply.

"So what's your gripe anyway?"

"I don't like it."

"He doesn't like it! Big deal. But I have an assignment and this is my job; so if you don't mind, step aside."

"Biff, please," Kay said, shocked the way the conversation drifted.

"Now that I got that settled, let's continue, Kay," Biff said.

"What, if I may be so bold to ask, is Miss Thompson's role in your photo assignment?" asked Mac.

"She's my model."

"I see."

It was the way he said it. He didn't see. He didn't see at all. Kay wanted to run to him and throw her arms around him.

"You will not be allowed to enter that area back there or photograph that patient," Mac said. "Haitians aren't the only people in the world who don't care to have their pictures sold abroad for someone else's profit."

"What's your hang-up, man?" Biff asked.

"Biff, please," Kay interceded. "This is not for profit," she protested, "for anyone's profit."

"And no one's benefit?" asked Mac.

"The clinic's."

"And not the model's," he said cynically.

"You don't understand," Kay said.

"You bet I don't understand. I don't understand how I was fooled, or maybe I do." He walked away.

"Mac, wait, please," Kay begged.

"Look, Kay, are we or aren't we going to finish this shoot? I only need a couple more shots."

"Well..."

"And to show you there are no hard feelings between us, I'll patch it up with your lover boy."

"He's not my lover!" Kay said angrily.

"I'll talk to him afterwards and explain. Come on, let's finish."

Reluctantly, Kay turned to the rear of the clinic and entered the ward where the patient lay.

"Can't you do something that looks nurse-like? Maybe give him a hypo for his pain?"

"Don't be ridiculous. Of course, I can't. If that's the kind of shot you want, I'll call one of the Haitian nurses over."

"Yeah, but she won't look half as sexy as you in a uniform. Forget it."

"Didn't I tell you two I don't want this man photographed?" Mac caught them completely unawares. "Why are you taking advantage of him?"

"You're making my assignment extremely difficult," Biff said.

"And you're making my life difficult," Mac said and left.

"How about some pictures of the nurses' station instead," Kay suggested.

"All right, since that guy wants to be such a sorehead. I suppose that will have to do. Hey, he just drove away," Biff said. "Let's take that patient shot, anyway," as they returned once again to the rear of the clinic.

"Get that bandage over there on the table and act as if you're going to change his dressing. That's fine. We'll shoot one more. That's it. I'll get the nurse's station on the way out. Sit at the desk and be the model for me, but don't look at the camera. Can you inspect some charts in your hand? Good." The shutter clicked a couple of times. "These photos should be perfect. I'll give you a lift back."

A deep sense of foreboding engulfed Kay as they headed for the hotel. She should have told Mac or perhaps warned him in advance about the pictures. But he was so arbitrary about his beliefs on clinic publicity, would it really have made any difference. He never would have consented.

"Who's the guy who's throwing his weight around?" Biff broke in on her thoughts.

"He's an M.D., Dr. MacDonald."

"So what? Does he own the place?"

"No, but he has been here the longest of any member of the staff."

"And what kind of a fancy salary does he pull?"

"He doesn't get one cent. This is all volunteer."

Biff hadn't even put the car in park when Kay flung open the door and hurried towards the hotel entrance.

There was a note for her at the desk. "It's too late for anything." There was no signature. There didn't have to be. The meaning, clear, absolute, unequivocal. Nothing more to be said Her options were sealed.

Biff, close behind, put his arm around her. "You look like you just lost your best friend."

She nodded.

"Sorry I loused up your day. We were gone for only about two hours, so why couldn't he wait? What was the rush?"

Biff was right. What was the rush? He could have waited if he had wanted to be with her. She ached. Her head was beginning to throb. The excitement she had anticipated about going to Milot was gone. So was her vitality, drained. Mac didn't understand. He was jumping to all sorts of conclusions. She so looked forward to being with him today, all day. Damn Biff anyway, screwing up her life again.

"Maybe you and I can do something today," Biff said.

Kay started to protest.

"Kay, don't be foolish. Your boyfriend has flown the coop and you can't stay inside the hotel all day. Tell me, what's there to do in a burg like this on a Sunday?"

Kay repressed a smile.

"Did you ever hear of a place called Sans Souci?" Biff asked.

Kay shook her head.

"Why don't we take off, see that, and in the evening we can have dinner at the Grand Hotel Oloffson and I'll drive you back here. Don't dress up; just change into your jeans, if you want."

She nodded dumbly. She didn't know what she was agreeing to. Slowly she climbed the steps to her room. Instead of removing her uniform, she sat on the bed, bewildered. How could she go out and enjoy herself at a time like this. The train of events that had transpired stupefied her.

"Kay, what's keeping you?" Biff banged on the door. "Open up. You're not even changed yet."

"Biff, I don't think I should leave."

"Of course, you should. It'll be good for you to get away from this place for a while. Do I have to dress you?"

"Biff, don't come near me."

"You need a little loving to give you some steam."

"Biff, I'm warning you. Stay away from me."

"You don't know what you're missing."

"If you can't behave yourself, I'm not going."

"You have nothing to fear but fear itself."

"I'll be down shortly."

She changed quickly into the beige jeans and brown and white poplin blouse she had planned to wear to Milot with Mac and left her room.

"That's more like it," Biff said, inspecting her, and leading her towards his car.

They traversed the village of Milot, past cottages shrouded in the curved ridges of corrugated iron till they came to a shell of what had once been a palace, the length of a city block.

"The place looks like it has been bombed out," Biff said. "According to the tourist folder, this was once called the Versailles of Haiti. Hard to believe, isn't it, when it's roofless, bricks faded."

Kay wandered aimlessly through the ruins.

"This must have been some pad, years ago, with ballrooms, banquet halls, private apartment. Henri Christophe knew how to live even back in those days."

"Biff, would you mind taking me back to my hotel?"

"Hey, I thought we were going to do some sight-seeing."

"I don't feel well."

"We can stop at the Oloffson and I'll get you some hot chicken soup and put you to bed."

"That's not funny," she said. "Now look, I cooperated with you on your pictures and the least you can do is to do what I want."

Biff shrugged. "OK, OK, I'll take you back, if that's what you want."

"Thank you."

"Is he really worth moping about?"

"Shut up, Biff."

"I've got a little gift for you to show you how much I appreciate your helping me out today."

"Why, Biff, how thoughtful of you. Louis Vuitton gloves?"

"That's right, my love. Just to show you how much I care."

"But Vuitton doesn't make gloves."

"A joke, my love."

"Is that how you care?"

"Sure," Biff said, tweaking her under the chin. "Something special. How many of your lovers can really afford to give you gloves by Louis Vuitton?"

"Especially, when they don't exist," Kay said.

"You got it."

"Sure look authentic with the logo and petaled flowers, white with black center and black with white center. The same logo that's on my luggage."

"They ought to look authentic. Costs 1100 francs in Europe."

"Did you pay . . . ?"

"Not I," Biff said, chuckling, "but people who aren't half as smart as you."

"Don't bother walking me to the door," Kay said, when the car stopped at the hotel.

"I'll send you a copy of the brochure once the photos are published."

Kay hurried into the hotel, ran up the stairs, and into her room. Then she flopped on the bed and wept. She'd lost him. Her heartache was bitter. She dozed off and awakened hours later to loud knocking. It was dark outside. She had had no lunch or dinner, but she didn't care to eat.

The knocking persisted, and for a moment, she was slightly disoriented, trying to figure out what had happened, why she had slept the way she did. Then she remembered and her heartache became painful once again.

"Kay, are you in there? Open up."

She couldn't believe it. It was Mac. Gratefully, she ran to the door, but as soon as he entered, she knew things were wrong. He didn't have to rage at her. It was there in his face. His jaw was rigid and that once wonderfully full mouth had become a grim line. But it was the eyes that told the story; they were the color of slate and hard.

"Now that you stood me up, do you want to give me an explanation?"

"I'm sorry, but I thought I'd be gone for only an hour."

His face remained unresponsive to her apology. "But it was for a good cause, so that's one consolation," Kay said.

"Whose cause—yours?"

"I'm trying to raise money for the clinic."

"Just like that, flouncing around like . . . like a model."

Where oh where was that gentle solicitude she loved? "You don't believe me, do you?" Kay knew she was pleading for reason. "You think I'm making up a story."

"Whatever you want to call it." He didn't get the message.

"Is that what you think?"

"What did you think I'd think, using the clinic as an excuse to parade your charms and promote your career as a model?"

"You read the letter from Clinics, International. There's nothing more to explain because it's the truth."

"You were modeling, weren't you, although I don't know why you were wearing a uniform and why you needed Clinics, International as an excuse to exploit the Haitians."

"But it's not an exploitation."

"That's what you say. The clinic doesn't need any publicity. I told you that before. It stands on its own merits. These poor Haitians come here for medical help and not to have their faces plastered in every magazine in the United States."

"But the clinic needs medicines, bandages, larger quarters, you said that yourself. And you can't do that on merit alone."

"You should have gotten clearance from me first, if this were a legitimate setup, instead of sneaking around with that photographer."

"I wasn't sneaking around, as you so quaintly put it. You saw us."

"I saw you, all right. With your old boyfriend."

Her tongue froze to the top of her mouth. Her voice, when she found it, was barely above a whisper. "What did you say?"

Then he spied the fake Vuitton gloves on the desk. "Where did you get these?" He picked up the gloves, examining them in his hands. "Where did you get these?" he demanded.

"Biff gave them to me after the shoot."

"Do you have more of these?" he asked.

"No."

"Now do you want to tell me the truth why you're really here in Haiti?"

"There's nothing to tell and I refuse to repeat the denials you have heard before."

"I see." He continued to scrutinize each of the gloves, rolling them over, studying them. "How much is he paying you to peddle these?"

"Who?"

"Your boyfriend."

"Get out of here."

"You're damned right I'll get out of here." He strode angrily to the door, throwing the gloves at her.

For several minutes, she sat and stared at the door after he left. She couldn't believe this was actually happening to her. This was the man she loved. He had blown everything way out of proportion. He refused to accept any of her explanations. Then she began to wonder. Did he provoke this as his chance to free himself of any commitment?

She picked up the gloves from the floor. What did he see that he kept turning and examining? Then it dawned on her. He recognized these as fakes and he thought she was smuggling counterfeit brands into the U.S.. For a moment, she didn't know whether she should laugh or cry. It was outrageous. Should she chase after him and tell him the real story about the gloves? What was the use? He wouldn't believe her anyway.

· · · ·

Monday morning Kay went down to breakfast earlier than usual, hoping to avoid Mac or anyone else in the dining room. She sipped her coffee slowly and munched on a piece of croissant. Her nerves were less frayed because she had managed to sleep on and off during the night, but deep within her, she hurt. Her love for him, pure and unalloyed, had been twisted and abused. She loved him hopelessly, desperately, impossibly.

"There you are." Kay's thoughts faded abruptly. Ruth dropped into the chair opposite. Her face was contorted into an expression of dislike. Anger seethed below the surface. Overt hatred masked any pretense of friendliness.

"I knocked on your door and couldn't understand where you were, especially, when I saw the jeep outside and knew you and Mac were still here. I didn't think you'd be brazen enough yet to spend the night in Mac's room."

"Is there something wrong?" asked Kay, confused by Ruth's unexpected attack.

Ruth laughed bitterly. "There sure is."

"What?"

"You. You're wrong."

Kay blinked in amazement. "I don't understand."

"Do you have an international driver's license?"

"Yes, I do."

"Then how come you had to have Mac drive you back here from Port-au-Prince."

"The road is bad."

"Is that so? It's the same road that you took to Port-au-Prince. Mac told me you were afraid to drive on that road."

"Ruth, Mac was free. He said you were staying an extra day to check on a couple of patients for him."

"I didn't stay that extra day. I didn't have to."

Why, thought Kay, because there weren't any patients?

"Then, on top of everything," Ruth said, "I got a flat tire, about a block from the hotel. I had to walk back and I had everyone here looking for Mac. No one could find him. Strange, wasn't it? He finally showed and got things moving again. You wouldn't know anything about that, would you?"

"Hardly."

"That's what I thought. That's all right because your play days are numbered."

What was she talking about?

"You needn't be surprised. I know exactly the kind of

woman you are. First you went after Jim. The fact that he was engaged didn't stop you, did it? Then when you got bored with him, Mac became fair game. Oh, you were clever the way you turned on the charm."

Kay looked at her, dumbfounded at the transformation of someone she once regarded as a friend. Was this the same Ruth who had first welcomed her so eagerly?

"Why don't you go away, Kay? Go away and let us work out our own lives, ourselves."

"You really want him, don't you," said Kay.

"He's mine. I've invested too much effort and energy in this man and I'm not about to let go. Stay away from Mac. You hear?"

"And if I don't?"

"You will because in another week when I've returned to Boston, we'll be announcing our engagement."

She rose from her seat. "I'll see you at the clinic. Tell Mac I'm taking my own car."

Kay sat there, stunned. The stubborn fact remained. How could she have been so dim-witted she couldn't see through him. She stared at the plate before her. There was one last morsel of croissant before her, but she couldn't finish it if her life depended on it.

"Are you through with your breakfast yet?" Mac strode impatiently into the dining room. Kay nodded. "Well, snap into it, will you? I haven't got all day."

Kay got into the jeep, making a point of keeping well to the right of him and ignoring him. She stared at the passing scene, anything to avoid talking to him.

To trust—isn't that what love is all about? Tears pricked the corners of her eyes. How could she ever think of loving a man like this, of building a life with him?

Mac pulled into his parking space at the clinic. Kay opened the door.

"Kay, wait a minute. I have a few things to say to you." She turned towards him. There was no remorse on his face, only seriousness. "I'm leaving for Boston Thursday and I want you to come with me."

Want. That's all he can think of. He never said he was sorry for the accusations he had hurled at her last night. Want, then use, then discard.

Kay shook her head.

"Don't say no yet. Think about it. I want you with me, Kay."

Cut and dried. That's it. No love, no caring, no thank you.

He stroked her cheek. She leaned away from him. Kay felt two strong arms around her and Mac's magnetic pull to him. His mouth swooped down on her, devouring her. She knew she was incapable of resisting him.

"Let me go. Stop it." She pushed her hands against his chest and wrenched herself free.

"Since when don't you like my kisses? Do I really have to sell myself to you at this stage of the game?"

So this is now a game. She wouldn't have known. Thanks for telling it like it is.

Now was the time to tip him off about the conversation she'd had with Ruth. She couldn't. She wouldn't know where to begin. It was too painful.

"I'm not going with you. I can't."

"Why?"

Tell him the truth. Didn't his forthcoming engagement to Ruth mean anything to him?

"Biff made me an offer."

"And that just about clinches everything, I suppose."

"Yes."

"You sure throw a mean curve ball, lady."

Kay studied her hands in her lap.

"Here's where you get off, Miss Thompson."

Kay left the jeep without a word.

Mac watched her walk to the clinic door. He wanted to call out to her to come back. He wanted to say, "I didn't mean what I said. Forgive me, Kay." He wanted to, but he didn't. Instead, he sat in the jeep and remained silent, thinking, but not acting.

She'd never forgive him and certainly never listen to his feeble apologies and excuses, which came too late. What could he say? Things had changed and he'd had time to think? That would be corny. Face it, he thought, he'd gotten what he deserved.

The clinic door opened and Ruth ran over to him. "Mac, are you all right?"

"Sure, sure."

"Why are you sitting in the jeep? What are you waiting for? A gilded invitation to join us inside?"

"You're right. I should get in there before I'm faced with a bottleneck. Let's go."

He put his arm around her and they walked together towards the clinic entrance.

Chapter 9

Kay steered clear of Ruth as much as she could. Her heart was breaking in two. She was glad there was little occasion to wallow in self pity, since the patient load was a heavy one.

Mac was businesslike and crisp, speaking to her only when necessary and addressing her as Miss Thompson, which caused even Jean-Pierre to raise an eyebrow.

All day she moved listlessly. She did everything she was supposed to do in helping the patients and keeping records, but her heart wasn't in it. She didn't feel rejected or jilted, just kind of letdown and alienated. Since Mac thought she was going away with Biff, there wasn't much more to be said.

At lunch Jim told Kay he was going home on Wednesday. "Too bad I wasn't here on Sunday. I missed the fireworks."

"What?" she asked.

"That photographer who was snapping pictures of the clinic. Kay, I got to hand it to you, you sure get around."

"Who told you," she asked.

"One of the optometrists."

"What else did he tell you?"

"That Mac was mad about the whole thing. Was he?"

"Unreasonably so."

Jim lowered his voice. "That guy was lucky Mac didn't break his camera."

"Where were you on Sunday?" Kay asked.

"Since this was my last weekend, Jean-Pierre and I rented a boat."

Out of the corner of her eye, Kay saw Jean-Pierre emerge from the clinic. He scanned the backyard. "Kay," he called, motioning to her, "can I see you?"

"Will you excuse me, Jim." She gathered up her lunch refuse and followed Jean-Pierre back into the clinic.

"What is it, Jean-Pierre?"

"Nicole's mother is here and wants to see you."

"Did something happen to Nicole?"

"She won't say a thing to me until she sees you."

The three of them huddled in a corner as Jean-Pierre translated a plea to Kay from Nicole's mother. Nicole became ill a day ago, is feverish, and keeps asking for Kay-Kay. Would she, could she, come?

Jean-Pierre waited for Kay's reply.

"Tell her I'll come after work tonight."

"Do you think that's wise, Kay?" Jean-Pierre asked, before relaying her answer.

"Whether it's wise or not, I don't know, but when Nicole feels so lonesome, I have to go because she considers me a friend."

"After all, she does have a mother and grandmother who care for her," Jean-Pierre said. "She's not exactly an orphan."

"Tell Nicole's mother I'll be there."

Kay walked over to her station. She wondered if a doctor were attending Nicole. There was very little she could do for the child except to hope that her visit would cheer her. She couldn't offer her anything else.

She hesitated. Maybe she should seek Mac's counsel.

That would be pointless. After her conversation with him this morning, he undoubtedly wanted nothing to do with her and probably couldn't care less what she did.

She didn't want to disappoint Nicole. The fact that the mother came all the way down to the clinic to seek her out convinced Kay that her presence was necessary for Nicole's well-being.

She watched and waited when Mac had given her the last patient card to file and he had returned to his examining room. Then Kay tapped Jean-Pierre on the arm and they scurried away.

As they headed up the mountains towards Nicole's house, Jean-Pierre grew adamant about remaining with her. "I refuse to listen to any arguments. I'm accompanying you there and I'm going to stay with you. "

"But, Jean-Pierre, it's silly. I mean I appreciate it and all that, but who knows how long I will have to be with Nicole."

"Don't give me any hassles. Stay as long as you want, but I'm going to wait with you. Remember what happened last time I didn't wait for you at the clinic? Dr. Mac was frantic about you and sore with me."

"I doubt if he'd feel that way now," Kay replied. "I thought you were taking your girlfriend out to dinner tonight."

"I am, but I already called her and told her I'd be a trifle late, so you see, it's settled. No more discussion."

"It's not settled," Kay said. "I've got a better idea. I'll take the bus back. There is a bus that runs by Nicole's house, isn't there?"

"Yes, but . . ."

"No buts about it. It's decided."

"Never underestimate the power of a woman." Jean-Pierre grinned at her. "In that case, let me show you where the bus stops."

They were at the top of the rise that led to Nicole's house.

"See where that beak juts out," Jean-Pierre said, pointing to a jagged tooth of rock, "that's your landmark, Kay. Directly below that is where the bus will pick you up. The last bus that goes to Port-au-Prince—that's the one that will stop at the hotel—is 9:00 o'clock, so give yourself plenty of time to get down because there are a lot of holes and depressions in the side of the hill."

"I'll see you tomorrow," he said, as Kay got out of the car.

She walked towards Nicole's house and knocked at the door, calling out, "*Hono,*" as she'd heard Jean-Pierre and Mac do. Nicole's mother opened it, responding with "*Respe,*" and beckoned her to enter.

Nicole was lying on a mat in the center of the small room, her doll next to her. Kay knelt at her side and stroked the child's forehead, which did feel unusually warm.

"Kay, *amie.*"

"Yes, you dear child, I'm your friend."

The mother remained standing as she watched Kay. If only she could speak to the woman, Kay thought. To suggest an aspirin for Nicole to break the fever. She was sorry she hadn't had Jean-Pierre stop in and translate.

Kay hummed a favorite lullaby of hers when she was a child. Little Nicole closed her eyes and soon fell asleep. Kay rose and tiptoed to the door. Then she saw the boxes at the other end of the room. She stepped back to investigate.

There were six of them, all open, revealing frames. She scooped up an armful and sat down on the floor to examine them more closely. Designer frames: Sophia Loren, Diane von Furstenberg, Christian Dior. All counterfeits, too.

Where did Nicole's mother get them? Was she going to sell them at the Iron Market? She'd have to make several trips down the mountain. She could never manage these boxes alone.

Kay scooped up another armful from a second box. Ray-Bans this time. How to get these to Jim? Face it, she couldn't,

There was just no way. She had no transportation. Nothing. Certainly, Nicole's mother wasn't going to help.

Then, without warning, Nicole's mother leaned over and with both hands gathered up the frames in Kay's lap and dropped them back in their box.

"*Non,*" she said. "*Non,*" she repeated herself, pointing to the door for Kay to leave.

Came in as a friend, Kay thought, and now leaving as an enemy. Wait till Jim hears of this cache she discovered.

She looked up at the sky for a sliver of moonlight to guide her. Even the stars were lost in the inky expanse of the heavens. She tried to figure out in which direction she should be going. She recalled that she'd have to go downhill to catch the bus. Well, that was a good start.

Why, oh why, didn't she think to bring a flashlight with her? How could she be so stupid as not to carry some kind of illumination? She made her way down the hill awkwardly, keeping a wary eye out for any potholes that might loom before her suddenly and threaten her equilibrium, despite the fact that she couldn't see much of anything.

She looked behind her and squinted. Was that the figure of a man crouched low? But why? Her imagination was running away with her.

She turned around to see a dim figure detach itself from the shadows of the house. Where did he come from? The figure sprang to life, slightly stooped, and darted towards her. Whoever it was, he'd seen her leave Nicole's house. It was as if he lay in ambush for her.

A black hood covered his head. Then he was behind her. She tried to crawl away from him. Her frantic breathing echoed in her ears as she moved to scramble further from her would-be assailant.

Then, he pushed her, hard. In that split instant she did not scream. She couldn't produce any sound other than a low moan from her throat because she was too terrified.

A sense of sliding into oblivion seized her. She continued to fall, powerless to do anything to help herself, until a thud broke the descent, depositing her finally in a depression farther down the hillside. She swiveled her head around. Her pursuer had already vanished.

A sharp pain radiated from her ankle up the calf of her leg. She pulled her leg out of the hole and attempted to raise herself to a standing position. The pain was excruciating and she knew she'd never make it. The only way she could get out of this mess would be to push herself along, dragging the injured leg.

That would be a fruitless effort. Aside from the fact it would take her forever and a day to get to any help like that, by leaving the area she might be making it more difficult for her rescuers to find her.

She was sure there'd be rescuers. She had to hope that someone would come. If she weren't found tonight, her absence at the clinic in the morning should rally someone. Mac would save her.

Would he? How could she be so sure about him anymore? But if he and Ruth had gone out for the evening and came back late, he'd never know. Jean-Pierre wouldn't know she was gone until the next day when she didn't report to work.

Jean-Pierre was the only one who knew she was here. She wondered. Did he push her? But why would Jean-Pierre resort to such a tactic? If he needed money for his education and was desperate, he knew about the designer frames in Nicole's house. Recalling how quickly her assailant had disappeared, she was positive that he had entered Nicole's home, since that was the only dwelling nearby.

She felt sick, nauseated. She might have to spend the entire night on this slope. The temperature would probably drop later and she didn't have a blanket or anything to cover herself.

Gloomily, she saw the bus coming around a bend in the road, the bus she was supposed to take back to the hotel. She sat there, half lay. Her ankle was throbbing. She had no way of knowing whether it was a sprain or a break. But what she began to experience was a surge of pain that oscillated in intensity as it rippled through her ankle and up into her calf.

As long as she lay still she was able to control the waves of pulsations, but when she moved her leg, the movement triggered such a spurt of agony she wanted to cry out. The night air chilled her and she shivered. She was cold and stiff and just plain miserable.

She'd never be able to stand on that leg. The best she could do was to stay where she was and hope that someone, anyone might begin to look for her soon, very soon.

Weariness rapidly overtook her and she drifted off to sleep She didn't know long she slept, but she awoke when she felt strong arms cradle her and heard a familiar voice, filled with concern, "Kay, dearest Kay, are you all right?" She was afraid to open her eyes and find herself dreaming.

"Kay, speak to me, please." Then Kay felt her lips lightly kissed.

Slowly, she opened her eyes and looked at Mac. "Put me down. I can walk," she protested.

"If you can walk, why did you wait for a rescuer?"

He carried her in his arms to the jeep and gently lowered her onto the passenger seat. Now she had a chance to examine herself. There was a cut on her arm where she had tried to cushion her fall. Her leg was also grazed. Her uniform was torn and dirty, her stockings, ruined, and her shoes, badly scuffed.

"I'm glad I found you," Mac said. "If it hadn't been for Jean-Pierre stopping at the hotel on his way home to tell me you'd be late for dinner because you were at Nicole's, I wouldn't have searched for you. I had made plans to go out this evening."

"Don't let me keep you, Doctor." She felt sick.

"Kay, don't say that."

"Why shouldn't I?"

"I know you're upset."

Upset? If he only knew how upset she was.

"Jean-Pierre said you would take the bus back to the hotel, so I postponed my evening plans till later."

"Am I supposed to thank you for that?"

"When you didn't get off," he continued, ignoring her comment, "I knew something must have happened to you."

"Bully for you."

"Do you want me to turn around and drop you off back at the hillside again?" Kay glowered at him. "We're almost at the clinic and we'll fix you up so you'll be good as new."

Good as new, except for a broken heart, she thought.

"Here we are. I'm going to carry you into the clinic."

"No, you're not."

"Yes, I am and don't be obstinate," he said, gathering her in his arms. "Besides, how often do I get the chance to carry a beautiful girl over the threshold?"

Mac placed her on one of the beds in the ward. Her ankle really ached now.

"Let me take a look at this," he said, as he removed her shoe. "Take off your hose."

She swung her legs around the other side of the bed, away from him. She rolled down her pantyhose, kicking them off into a heap on the floor.

"Now lie back on the bed," Mac ordered. He hiked her uniform well above her knees. Kay yanked her dress down, her fingers unwilling to withdraw from the hem. Then she tried to curl her leg beneath her.

"Kay, stop it! How can I examine you? Your sudden modesty with me least becomes you. I've seen you at the beach when you've had fewer clothes on." He planted a kiss on her neck. "So what are you ashamed of?"

"I'm not the one who has to be ashamed."

"I don't know what that's supposed to mean and at the moment, I don't care," he said, forcibly thrusting her hands aside. "Your leg has some cuts and bruises and will have to be washed."

"No."

"I'm going to take a look at that leg and ankle whether you like it or not. I'm a doctor, Kay."

"But you're an eye doctor," she declared.

"Stop being childish. I know how to cleanse a wound." Kay pushed his hands away.

"Kay, do you want me to call one of the nurses in here to hold you down?"

Kay relented, withdrawing her hands.

He gave his attention to cleaning the wounds on her leg and arm. She flinched at the sting of the antiseptic.

He pressed firmly on an area near the injured ankle. "Does this hurt?" he asked.

"Yes," Kay said, stifling a sob.

Mac took her in his arms. "Kay, I wouldn't hurt you. You know that." He kissed her neck.

She wanted to bawl right then and there, not so much because of her ankle but because she knew she'd lost him.

"I can't tell if your ankle is broken," he said, "without an x-ray."

"Oh."

"You'd have to go to Port-au-Prince for that."

"I don't want to go."

"Tell you what—we'll put an elastic bandage on it and see how that works out. Maybe it's only a sprain. Then, depending on how you feel, you can hobble around here. Cheer up. It's not the end of the world. I'll see you in the morning." He leaned over and brushed his lips against hers. "I'll give you a couple of pain pills so you can get a good night's rest."

He left and returned shortly with a bottle of pills and a glass of water. "See you tomorrow morning, Kay. Sleep well. I'll have one of the nurses bring you a surgical gown."

. . . .

Kay was awakened the next morning by her first visitor, Ruth.

"You think you can get Mac back this way, don't you, by playing on his sympathies? I don't believe that your ankle is sprained or even broken."

"Too bad if you don't."

"Why did you go to Nicole's?"

"Her mother said she was feverish and calling for me."

"Since when do you make house calls?"

"Well, the child was ill," Kay began.

"What do you know Nicole had? Suppose she had a contagious disease and then you come back here and infect everyone. You didn't think about that, did you?"

"I comforted Nicole once before when she was distressed, and I thought I could help her again."

"Help her! That's a joke. How? If she's so feverish, as you say, then her mother should take her to the general medical clinic nearby. Both the grandmother and mother are aware of the medical facilities available to them."

"What do you mean if she's so feverish?" asked Kay. "Of course, she was."

"How would you know? You're not a doctor or a nurse, either. Did you have a thermometer with you?"

"Are you insinuating that I went out and fell in that hole so that I could get Mac's attention?"

"Do you have a better explanation?"

"Someone pushed me."

"That's a good one."

Kay was disgusted and turned her head away from Ruth.

"You always have to be in the limelight, don't you? And if you can't have an audience, you make one. I heard about your modeling on Sunday. What were you wearing, a bikini? Must have created quite a sensation."

"I was wearing my uniform," Kay said, sickened by the accusation, "and I didn't do it for myself. I was doing it for the clinic."

"Good causes are a dime a dozen, honey. If your cause

is Mac, then I suppose that's as good as any. Since you claim to be so responsive to the needs of the clinic, you also might think of something else. How are we going to replace you today? We're shorthanded as it is."

"I'll get up and work," Kay said, partially rising from the bed.

"Our little martyr, ready to earn her Oscar for an Academy Award performance." Ruth left as unceremoniously as she had come.

"How's the patient today?" asked Mac, entering seconds later.

"I think I'll get up."

"Feel well enough to get out of bed?"

"I know you'll be busy today and I'm sure you and Jean-Pierre could use some assistance."

"I'll only be here in the morning. Then I have to go to Port-au-Prince."

"When are you coming back?"

"Late Wednesday afternoon. I'd return sooner but there are a couple of people I have to pick up."

"Oh."

"Don't look so glum." He leaned over and kissed her. "I'll be back tomorrow in time for the party. Ruth will tell you all about it," he said, already taking his leave.

One of the Haitian nurses brought Kay her uniform, which had been mended and laundered for her. Kay was touched by the act. The nurse rewrapped the elastic bandage around the ankle.

"One good turn deserves another," the nurse said. "Everyone on the staff has heard of your own kindness towards Nicole and how you took the time to visit her. Washing and darning your uniform was the least we could do."

Dressed at last, Kay eased her bare foot into her shoe, wincing a little when the sore limb supported her briefly, and she wobbled and tottered down the hall.

Jean-Pierre saw her coming and rushed to her aid. Slowly, she lowered herself on the chair he pulled out for her.

"I knew I shouldn't have listened to you last night."

"Don't blame yourself, Jean-Pierre. If you had waited, there would been two casualties on that hill instead of one."

"I bet you didn't have a flashlight with you."

"You're right about that."

"I had one in the car." He shook his head incredulously.

"Jean-Pierre, did you leave the area as soon as you had left me?"

"Sure, why?"

"I didn't fall down that hill. I was pushed." He seemed visibly upset.

"Did you recognize who it was?"

"He was wearing a hood over his head."

Was that relief she saw on Jean-Pierre's face?

"Why would anyone do that to you?"

"I don't know. But I did find six boxes of copycat designer frames in Nicole's house."

"Ray-Bans, too, like before?"

Kay nodded.

"Maybe that guy coming to make a pickup felt you might interfere."

"But how did he know I was there and how would he know that I'd be interested in copycat designer frames?"

"I think you should mention this to Dr. Mac."

"Mention what to me?" asked Mac, coming in on the tail end of the conversation.

"Kay said she was pushed down that hill," Jean-Pierre said.

"Why didn't you tell me that before?"

"I didn't want to make a big deal out of it," Kay said.

"Anything that happens to you is a big deal to me. Jean-Pierre, can you hold down the fort for a minute? Kay, I want to talk to you in my office. Need some help walking?"

"No, I can manage."

. . . .

Then she told him about the box of designer frames and other boxes containing Ray-Bans. Kay watched his reaction as she spoke. Was his concern merely for her?

"Isn't that stupid," he said, "dragging the poor people into the operation. Do you have an idea how many frames were in the one box, each box?"

"No."

He grew pensive. "Kay, you could have been seriously injured." He reached for her hand. "I don't want anything to happen to you," he said, kissing her tenderly on the mouth. "Be careful where you go, please." What she had just told him, coupled with her near accident, made his caution sensors stand on end. He didn't want to alarm her unduly. Maybe he was over-reacting. But when it came to her, he just couldn't be objective.

"I think I better help Jean-Pierre," Kay said at last, pulling away from him.

"Did you say you saw six boxes of copycat frames there? No more? Only six?"

Yes," Kay said, "but some of those boxes contained Ray-Bans, too. Counterfeit sunglasses." She made her way slowly down the hall.

"Are you sure you want to work today?" Jean-Pierre asked when she sat down.

"Why not? I'm not sick, only a sprained ankle, I hope. I don't think it's broken. If it were, I'm sure I couldn't walk on that foot. I don't have to stand. I can sit most of the time. I'll let you take the patients over to the exam room."

"All right, but if you decide you don't feel up to it, let me know. Doc's going to be here only in the morning anyway."

"I know. He told me."

When Mac emerged from his office with the first patient in tow, he stopped to talk to Kay.

"Your ankle isn't paining you, is it?"

She shook her head.

"Then why the tears? You know what? We'll elevate that leg for you so there won't be so much pressure." He returned to his office and brought a small stool. "Can you put your foot on this?" Was this Mac, the caring doctor or Mac, the caring lover? If only she knew. He had never asked if she'd known or recognized her attacker or why she thought she was attacked.

"That's better, isn't it?" The throbbing had stopped with her leg elevated. He smiled at her and called out to the next patient to follow him.

At noon Mac said good-bye to Kay and Jean-Pierre. "I'll see you tomorrow night. Jean-Pierre, keep an eye on Kay for me so she doesn't turn the other ankle."

To Kay he said nothing, but looked at her, his eyes aglow, his lips mouthing a "good-bye."

Jean-Pierre helped Kay get settled at a table in the backyard and brought her a sandwich. "I'm going to eat later, Kay, because I'll be working with Jim this afternoon and want to see what's going on in his department."

Kay removed her sandwich from the wax paper. The rear door of the clinic opened and out came Ruth. She marched purposefully towards Kay's table as if to do battle and sat directly across from her.

"Well, well, fancy meeting you here. Are you coming to the party tomorrow night, or should I ask, do you think you'll be well enough to come?"

Kay ignored the sarcasm. "Dr. Mac said I should ask you for the details. I don't know anything about them."

"That's a hot one, you're asking me. The staff is giving a party for us before we return to Boston."

"You're leaving, too?" Kay asked, fearful she was opening a Pandora's box.

"Why not? I had planned to go next week, but it seemed senseless to postpone the inevitable. Besides, two can go as cheaply as one. The party is not only a farewell party but kind of a prenuptial celebration." With unerring aim, Ruth let loose her wallop. "We'll be announcing our engagement."

Kay cried out in alarm as she stood to go, swaying a bit. She felt all the blood drain from her face.

"Why wait till we get back to Boston," Ruth continued, "to reveal our plans. This way everyone on the staff can share in the news."

Kay's legs could no longer sustain her and she collapsed helplessly into her chair. With a sense of anguished frustration, she realized the last few minutes had robbed her of the hope that she and Mac would settle their differences about what happened on Sunday.

Once she had grasped the truth and could no longer brush aside the growing doubt that had become a suspicion, everything seemed to fall into place. So this was how he was repaying her for his disapproval of Biff's photographing her. His impending engagement to Ruth was a cruel joke.

"Kay, did I forget to mention, you're invited to the party and you don't even have to bring a gift," Ruth said. "Jim is the only one who won't be present because he already made his plans to go home."

How she got through the rest of the day, she didn't know. Why didn't Mac tell her the truth? The fact he couldn't bring himself to face her, that he had to have Ruth enlighten her made her furious, furious that he had become an obsession in her life. He didn't know what love is, what it demands. Yet he had refused to accept any explanation of hers when she and Biff were working Sunday. She knew she would pay a high price for these past two weeks.

Sure, she told Mac that Biff had made her an offer, but that wasn't a marital offer. Furthermore, she hadn't said she had accepted. But she had to lie. How else could she have responded to Mac when Ruth told her they were going to announce their engagement upon their return to Boston.

Still, if Mac really wanted her, he would have pursued her without having to run to Ruth.

"You look very pale," Jean-Pierre observed, as she came towards him. "Maybe you should stay in tomorrow. Doc won't be back till evening and I'll be working with one of the optometrists, since Jim is leaving."

"I think I will." Her own plans were rapidly crystallizing in her mind. She knew she had to leave immediately. She would leave tomorrow with Jim, somehow, some way. She had no intentions of going to a party where Mac and Ruth would announce their engagement. That would be the ultimate outrage.

She would be gone tomorrow when he returned. That way she wouldn't have to face him. She knew he was lying to her. He must realize that. Yes, she was glad he thought Biff had tendered an offer. At least, she could leave Haiti with some shred of self respect.

"Don't forget the party for Dr. Mac and Ruth tomorrow night," Jean-Pierre said.

She hesitated only for a moment. She should say good-bye properly to Jean-Pierre. He had been kind to her, gracious, accommodating, but if she said good-bye to him, she'd have to do the same to the rest of the staff. Then her departure would no longer be secret. She turned around to wave to Jean-Pierre. She'd write him a note when she got home and hope he'd understand.

She limped over to Jim as he completed his paperwork. "You've got a passenger tonight," she said.

"Fine. First, I want to say good-bye to a few special people who have been so great to me while I was here."

Kay watched him walk over to Jean-Pierre, clasp his arm, and shake hands. Next Jim approached Ruth. "I wish both you and Mac the best in the world," he said.

That was all Kay had to hear. She hobbled in agony to the foyer where she waited patiently for Jim while he made the rounds through the rest of the clinic. It was Ruth all along and everyone knew it and she, the dumb little country girl, was an easy mark, dazzled by the big city doctor.

"Sorry to keep you waiting, Kay." Jim scrutinized her. "You don't like to say good-bye either, do you?" She knew her eyes were glistening with tears. Jim took her arm. "It's not really good-bye, you know, only so long. When Mary Ellen and I are married, we'll be seeing you often." He helped her get settled in his car.

"How's the ankle, by the way?"

"Better."

"Someone said you were pushed. Is that true?"

"Yes."

"By whom?"

"I don't know."

"How do you know you were pushed then?"

"I saw him come for me."

"What did he look like?"

"I don't know."

"You don't know who pushed you, but you saw him. You don't know what he looked like, but you saw him."

"He had a black hood over his face. But, Jim, I saw six boxes, all opened, of designer frames in Nicole's house."

"Ray-Bans, too?" Jim asked.

"Yes, and Nicole's mother was very upset when I tried to examine the fakes. I hope she isn't mixed up in this copycat operation."

"I don't think she is, but I think her house is a pickup point for the guy behind the scam. I bet he was the same guy who pushed you."

"Are you sure?"

"Quite sure. He's also the guy we expect to catch in our sting. In the end, we'll seize those copycat frames and Ray-Bans that you saw because they'll be in the guy's possession."

"Jim," she began quietly, "I want to go home with you tomorrow."

"Huh?"

"I mean I want to be on that plane with you."

"Why, all of a sudden? Your uncle sick or something?"

Kay did not confirm or deny the statement. She dropped her gaze to her folded hands in her lap.

When she didn't answer, Jim replied, "Sorry to hear

about that. I don't know if you can get a seat on my flight. You might have to be standby."

"I don't care, as long as I know I can leave some time tomorrow."

"It's that urgent, huh? Don't forget, though, we have a sting operation tomorrow morning before we board the plane."

"Did you make your contact?" she asked.

"Yup. One of the big muckety mucks running the illegal business called me and said he was definitely interested in what we had to offer and he'll be there. After the arrest is made, we'll take off."

As soon as Kay returned to the hotel, she called the airlines and considered it Fate when she learned there were seats still available. Next, she sent her uncle a telegram telling him when she'd arrive at County Airport so he could meet her. Then she went downstairs to have dinner with Jim.

"Think I'll order a good stiff drink tonight," Kay said.

"Scotch and soda," she told the waiter. "Jim, what about you?"

"Nothing for me." Jim looked at her sharply. "The place really gets to you, doesn't it?" She nodded, not daring to speak.

"Who knows," he said, "maybe some day you'll be back for a honeymoon. Then you can look up the old gang."

Kay mumbled a "maybe" and studied the menu, finally ordering a Salisbury steak and a salad, afraid that a heavy meal would only wreak greater havoc with a stomach that was already jumpy.

She concentrated on her food while Jim talked and talked, although her mind was miles away. Every once in awhile she looked up from her plate and uttered, "Hmm, that's right." It was almost a relief when they were through eating.

"Time to pack," Kay said.

"You've got all evening for that," Jim said. "Why don't

you relax a bit? You've had a harrowing day, what with your ankle."

"I like to get everything ready so that I don't have to rush around the last minute and then, forget something."

"A time nut, huh?" He laughed. "I'll see you tomorrow morning at 6:30. We'll have breakfast here, check our luggage at the airport, and head for the Olofsson to meet our parties."

For the next hour or so, she was so absorbed in folding clothes that she couldn't think of anything else. She didn't want to and knew that if she did stop her flurried activity she'd have too much time to think.

She looked around the room and remembered to take the ash tray she had bought her uncle. Then she saw the Haitian primitive, standing in the corner. She didn't have room for it. Mac could keep it. The painting had once meant a future, precious for both of them, or so she thought. She had romanticized it as an expression of what she felt was his love.

For him, it was a token of what? Another testimonial of another conquest? He paid for it and he could keep it, as far as she was concerned. She didn't owe him anything. She looked away from it, closed her suitcase, and the image of Mac's face appeared to her. She could close the suitcase and leave the island, but how would she ever shut him out from her life if she could so easily fill her mind with him now?

Chapter 10

Kay opened the door to her room and slid her suitcase out in the hall. Jim came quickly to her assistance. "Here, let me. How does that ankle feel?"

"Much better."

He placed her suitcase in the lobby. "Wait here. I almost forgot the most important cargo," he said, racing up the steps. He lugged two large boxes downstairs, placing them next to Kay's suitcase. "Watch these for me, will you, Kay? I've got two more to go."

"Should I know what's in there," she asked, pointing to them.

"I'll bring the rest of the bait down and stow it in the jeep and I'll let you see for yourself."

He bounded back up the stairs and carried down the remainder. "Now all you have to do, Kay, is watch these two while I load the first two. Then I'll come back for them and your luggage."

Jim hustled as if he were possessed, carting away the first half and dashing back into the hotel for the rest.

"Jim, I can carry my own suitcase."

"Are you sure?"

"Of course I'm sure."

"If you think so, that would be a big help."

Kay grabbed the handle of her suitcase and slowly walked out of the hotel.

"I'll take that from you," Jim said, as he placed it in the back of the jeep. "I want to show you something." He took one of the boxes and carefully opened a flap.

"Where did you get those?" asked Kay,

"From a very cooperative guy named Willoughby."

"All Ray-Bans?"

"Just this one box. The others are designer frames. Great bait for a big fish. You probably should familiarize yourself with some of the stage props we'll be using." He chuckled, opening the flaps of another box.

Kay picked up a Christian Dior and carefully examined it. "A genuine fake," she whispered. "The hinge."

Jim grinned at her. "I think I can use you in my next sting operation."

"Nothing doing. I'm going back to the farm."

"Too bad. You've got a great future in scams."

After checking their luggage at the airport, they drove to the Oloffson Hotel.

"So this is Haiti's Grand Hotel," Kay said, as Jim pulled into a parking spot. She got out of the jeep and stood back a ways to take it all in.

"I thought you had seen it before," Jim said, as he began to unload the boxes.

"No, how could I? I had heard about it, even back in the States. But I had no idea it was like this—so Victorian, with all that gingerbread. Where's our room?"

"We have a room reserved on the first floor," Jim said, "which reminds me—we better shake a leg and get all this stuff inside before our guests begin to arrive. I'll take these two heavier boxes first and then come out for the other two."

He carried the first load in and returned quickly for the remainder, beckoning to Kay, "Hurry." They had barely arranged the props in the room when two sharp raps on the door announced the first guests.

The American and Haitian who had called upon Mac at the clinic entered.

"Kay, may I introduce you to . . ." Jim started to say.

"Never mind," Kay interrupted, "we've already met. I know them."

"No, you don't. They're from Customs."

Kay's eyes widened; and she had thought Blue Eyes over there was a gangster. Hard to tell who was who without a program.

"Is Dr. MacDonald here yet," the Haitian asked Jim.

"No, and I don't think we'd be able to get him to come today."

"That's too bad. What do we have to do, issue a subpoena?"

"You might have to," Jim said. "He's leaving for Boston very soon."

Kay sat there, stunned. So Mac was mixed up in this as much as she feared. She'd never forgive him for that. She was glad she was leaving. She couldn't bear to see him in handcuffs.

Four loud knocks stopped the conversation that had ensued between Jim and the two Customs agents.

"I'll get it," Kay said, as she opened the door and found herself face to face with Biff.

"I thought you had to be in Chicago," she said.

"Something came up at the last minute."

"I'm sure." She glared at him. She wouldn't put anything past this guy.

Right behind Biff was the Haitian with the earring who had demanded Darvon. "Hi, gorgeous," he greeted her. "Remember me?"

"Only too well," Kay said.

"And what, may I ask, are you, of all people, doing here," Biff said.

"The same thing you are," Kay replied.

"Working a little sideline, eh? Smart girl. This is the way to go. How about joining up with me later?"

"I'll think about it."

"It's too hard for a lone female to work this racket by herself."

"Let me introduce you to a friend of mine," Kay said. "Jim, I'd like you to meet Biff."

"The photographer?" Those red eyebrows of Jim jumped up in disbelief before settling back into a poker face.

"Where did you hear about me?" Biff asked.

"Kay, of course."

Gleefully, Biff rubbed his hands together. "I'm anxious to see what you got in those boxes."

"Enough to make you a very rich guy," said Jim.

"That's what I like to hear."

"Kay," Biff said, "if I had known you were involved in this operation, too, I could have saved you a nasty fall down the hillside."

"So it was you!"

"Listen, a guy can't be too careful these days and I've got a big investment here. But it's all right, relax, you're OK now, I see. Everything's fair in love and war. I wasn't the only game in town. We could have linked up together a long time ago. I came for that pickup in that Haitian house and I thought you were muscling in on my deal. Can you blame me? Got to protect my interest, you know."

"Yeah, you're good at that," Kay said.

"I'd like to examine the merchandise first," Biff said, "before I put my money where my mouth is."

Jim moved the boxes of fake glasses over for his inspection. Biff dug into all four, grabbing at random.

"Yahoo! This is as good as gold. You got yourself a deal," and with that, he pulled out several hundred dollar bills to close the transaction. "Did you guys bid already," he asked, pointing to the three men and Kay.

"They did," Jim said, "but no one is willing to pay what you are."

"Too bad for them. Great for me. This will be more than worth the price of admission, what I'll eventually realize. Kay, think about what I said. My offer still stands. You can come with me and grow rich. You know where you can reach me, don't you?"

"No. You've left Iowa. Are you in Chicago?"

"Here's my calling card. Kay, it will be like old times again, having you with me and doing something that really pays. Got to hit the road now."

The two Customs agents remained seated, but wary, until Biff had removed all the boxes. Then, as he began loading the merchandise into his car, they sprang into action.

Kay slipped out, unobtrusively, and stood in the shadow of the hotel to witness the confrontation.

"So you want to get in on this now?" asked Biff. "Tough luck, guys. No way. You're too late."

"U.S. Customs," the American said. Kay saw him flip open his badge. "You're under arrest."

That's what she wanted to hear. She turned to reenter the hotel, but went over on her ankle, pitching her headlong in the grass, and caught Biff's eye.

"We're even now, aren't we, Kay?" he yelled, shaking a clenched fist at her, as she scrambled to her feet.

"Hey, hold still, buddy," the Customs agent said.

Kay heard the snap of the handcuffs. She expected to hear Biff follow through with a threat but none was forthcoming. She limped back into the hotel.

"What happened to you?" Jim asked.

"You're not going to believe this . . ."

"I know. You twisted the other ankle. You're OK, otherwise?"

Kay nodded. "Serves me right for eavesdropping."

"Too tempting not to, wasn't it?"

* * * *

Shortly after, Kay and Jim were airborne. Kay looked out of the window for the last time at the claw of Haiti, remembering vividly how she felt two weeks ago when she first arrived. How she believed she was dramatically changing the future course of her life.

The great clarion call that motivated her to volunteer for Haiti had netted her nothing. She had no recommendation for future employment as an optician. Not only did she lose that, but also the man she loved.

There were hills and mountains below, but her vision blurred. What did it matter to her where he was, where he went, whom he saw. She still had her opticianry training. No one could take that away from her, she thought grimly, and there was a shortage of parahealth professionals like herself.

However, she could use a recommendation. It wouldn't hurt, especially, if she were competing with another applicant for the same job.

She wouldn't dream of writing and seeking a letter from Ruth, for obvious reasons. Besides, Ruth was so vindictive, how could Kay trust her? As for asking Mac for a recommendation, Kay fought back the tears that sprang to her eyes. She wanted to keep her whereabouts secret. With such a shortage in the field, she might be able to skirt the thorny issue of references.

Why waste time thinking about someone who could never mean anything to her once she left the island and whose existence she'd have to completely forget by the time the plane touched down in Iowa. He had so often accused her of being a creature of impulse, implying she was what? Unreliable? Unstable? Maybe her feelings towards him, too, were unreliable and unstable.

"Tired?" Jim asked.

Kay nodded.

"You've been awfully quiet since we boarded. Anxious to get home?"

"Yes. Jim, what will happen to Biff?"

"He was caught negotiating for the fakes and will probably go to prison after a trial."

"And Mac?"

"Mac wasn't involved, ever involved. I told you that before."

"Then why were those Customs agents looking for him?"

"Remember, I mentioned how they had been supplying him with designer kits. They have more of them and want him to take them back to Boston with him."

"And that line about their having to get a subpoena out on him . . ."

Jim chuckled. "Strictly jaundiced bureaucratic humor. Where's your sense of humor?"

Not when it comes to Mac, she thought. "Do you know that other Haitian—the one with the earring?"

"He's a narc, a narcotics agent."

"What's his connection to the Tripwire operation?"

"Narcs are always on the lookout for drugs being smuggled into the U.S. in one form or another. He has been bringing Mac some counterfeit lens implants, so he can learn to distinguish them from the real ones."

Suddenly, she felt better and closed her eyes. But she couldn't sleep. She didn't want to pass the time chatting with Jim, either, so she kept her eyes closed.

A sense of desolation hit her. The pattern of her life will continue relentlessly, as if there had been no interruption at all until what? She didn't know. It was as if she were doomed to pick up the pieces of her life just as she had before, with no hope or letup in sight. Perhaps she would never be able to break out of the rut. Where was that proverbial light at the end of the tunnel? To her, it looked like nothing more than a train coming through. The thought depressed her even more.

"Kay, wake up. We're landing." Jim's voice broke into her reverie. "Got your seat belt fastened? It'll be good to be home again."

Once at O'Hare in Chicago, they boarded the plane for Iowa. Kay was the first to deplane at County Airport.

"Jim, thanks for everything."

"You're not mad at me anymore?"

"How could I be?"

"Take care," he said, and unexpectedly kissed her.

Kay walked down the ramp. She spotted her uncle immediately, a dissatisfied expression on his face as usual. She, too, felt dissatisfied. Instead of happiness at returning home, there was the deep seated feeling of being incomplete, unfinished. She was going to have to do something to get her life back on track again and stop thinking of Mac.

"Did you get whatever it was out of your system," her uncle gruffly greeted her. "You must have, else you wouldn't have lasted only a couple of weeks. I told you altruism is all right, but charity begins at home, my dear."

Kay blanched.

He eyed her. "Come to think of it, you don't look too good. Must have been the food, I suppose."

She needed a day to orient herself. "Jet lag," she told him. At least he seemed pleased she remembered him with the ash tray.

"What are your plans about finding a job?" That's all he can think of. He hasn't given me a chance to catch my breath, she thought, and he wants to know how I'm going to support myself, now that I've burned all of my bridges nicely behind me.

"In a day or so, I plan to drive over to the Placement Bureau at school to see what they might have."

"Your Haitian experience, brief as it was, should count for something."

Kay mumbled agreement. Yes, her Haitian experience should count for something. What? That she would be wary about falling in love again? That never again would she be deceived by a man who was interested only in toying with her emotions. Perhaps she should have stayed in Haiti and fought for Mac, Ruth be damned. She could have. Why didn't she?

She knew the reason. He never said the words she really wanted to hear. He wanted her. Whatever he wanted, he took. She should have known early in the relationship he was that kind of a man.

She'd lose herself in her work. Very therapeutic, Ruth had once told her. Heavens knows she needs to do something therapeutic. Ironic that the one time she was doing something for someone, her trip to Haiti to help others, would wreck her life, perhaps forever.

"Kay, you're not listening to me," her uncle admonished.

"Sorry, I must have been daydreaming."

"I was saying that I thought I'd give you a break and prepare the supper tonight because you'll take over in the kitchen soon for both of us."

There it is again—the same old pattern she had been trying so desperately to break, to extricate herself from. She had hoped that the work in Haiti would be her lifesaver.

"Don't fuss, Uncle Ted. I think I'll settle for a bowl of vegetable soup, scrambled eggs, and toast."

"That all?" he asked, amazed. "After traveling practically a whole day?"

"I'm afraid so."

After supper, Kay retired early. It felt good to be back in her own bed again, no doubt about it. Even weeping into her own pillow was comforting in a way. She closed her eyes and slipped into a sound sleep.

. . . .

The next morning Kay was in Hilldale at the Placement Bureau. The several vacancies on the bulletin board encouraged her. Miss Brownell, the director, remembered her.

"Welcome home, stranger. How was Haiti?"

"Fine," said Kay, anxious to proceed with a discussion

of available job opportunities. "I'm looking for a position now."

"We have two openings in Colorado, three in Arizona, one in Wisconsin, and one right here in Hilldale."

Here was the chance she was waiting for—to get away from Iowa, to go to some place like Colorado, where no one knew her, where she could begin a new life. Unfortunately, she wasn't ready to leave everything so neatly like that. That was too much like running away. She needed to sort out her life, temporarily, and analyze it before deciding to leave. She needed the solace of familiar surroundings around her for awhile.

"Can you tell me about the opening in Hilldale?" Kay inquired.

"Decided not to roam eh?" Miss Brownell said. "At this address downtown there is a Dr. Novak who is looking for an optician." She wrote the address on a card and handed it to Kay.

"Is he an M.D.?" Kay asked.

"Do you have any objections if he's not?"

"None at all."

"He's one of our busiest optometrists. Why don't you call him from here? You might be able to arrange an interview today."

When Kay phoned Dr. Novak, he suggested she come to see him within the hour.

"I don't suppose you have any idea how many are competing for this position, Miss Brownell."

"All I can tell you is that most of our grads want to use their optician certificate as a passport to a more glamorous location like New York City or San Francisco or Houston. You're a rarity, content to stay home and mend fences."

Kay turned to leave.

"You shouldn't be worried about competition," Miss Brownell said. "You have a strong academic record and you do have that experience bit in Haiti. Good luck to you."

Kay thanked her and left, but back in her car she sat

and sorted out her thoughts. If only she knew whether this was the right course to follow, or would this, too, turn out as another fool's errand, like Haiti.

The only way to find out was to get there. She put the key in the ignition, stepped on the accelerator, and drove off.

A short, stocky, balding man in his late fifties smiled warmly at Kay, introduced himself informally as Don Novak, and ushered her into his office. Kay handed him a copy of her resumé.

"Miss Brownell spoke to me while you were on your way over and told me you've been to Haiti working at the Eye Clinic."

"My stay was so short that I doubt you can consider it as relevant," Kay said, concerned he might ask for a reference.

"If you were there only a couple of days, it's noteworthy," he said kindly. His gray eyes smiled at her. "Who was the doctor you were working with?"

"Dr. MacDonald. Ian MacDonald."

"I don't believe I know him. Is he an optometrist?"

"No, an ophthalmologist."

"Then I wouldn't know him. I was in Haiti two years ago; but when I was there, there were no physicians around, only optometrists like myself. You and I are going to have to swap stories about our experiences down there. Do you know anything about cosmesis?" he asked, as he studied the resume before him.

"Yes, I do. That was one of the elective courses I took at Tech."

"Good. I need an optician with that background. My women patients appreciate that kind of assistance."

Kay peered into the four rooms that comprised the office suite. The earth tones of brown, beige, and taupe, mingling with an occasional chair in burnt orange furnished an attractive backdrop for an optometric setting. It was a bright, cheery atmosphere and she was sure she could feel comfortable here.

Dr. Novak watched her. "Any questions you want to

ask about the position? The job is yours, if you're still interested."

"Very much," said Kay.

"Can you start tomorrow? I know it's short notice, but my former optician left suddenly to join her husband, who is stationed in the army in California."

"I'd like to start right away."

"Good, the sooner the better."

Kay returned to the Placement Bureau to inform Miss Brownell that she had taken the job, then drove home. She bustled around getting supper ready. Just like old times, she thought ruefully. She was setting the table when the doorbell rang.

"Mary Ellen! How did you know I was back?"

"Jim told me you had returned with him and I simply had to drop by to say hello after leaving work. I'm working right here in Middleville as an optician."

"And I'm working in Hilldale," Kay said, "with Dr. Novak. He hired me this afternoon."

"Great! I'm glad you'll be around the area for awhile and I'm so glad you came back early from Haiti because we've decided to advance the wedding date."

"We've decided?"

"Well, I've decided," she said, a sly smile on her face.

"Are you up to your old tricks again, Mary Ellen?"

"Of course, I am. Wouldn't be any fun if I weren't."

"When's the big date?" Kay asked.

"End of next month."

"How does Jim feel about that?"

"He says it's OK with him. I've got a job working for a dream of a doctor and I can support Jim easily his last year of school."

Kay couldn't help but grin at Mary Ellen's bubbly enthusiasm as she jabbered away.

"Got to run, Kay, forgive me. Listen, I've gone ahead and ordered your bridesmaid gown. The gown will be delivered tomorrow afternoon. Try it on, check to see if it fits well so if there are any alterations to be done, we can attend to them in plenty of time. Don't forget. You're my maid of honor."

"How could I ever forget that?"

"I want to hear about your experiences in Haiti, but some other time when I'm not so rushed."

Kay nodded. Some other time, indeed, she thought, when the memory of it will have passed into oblivion. For the present, she felt like a shadow of her former self, a will of the wisp, hurrying here and there, looking for something, someone. She had to get Mac out of her mind. She went back into the dining room and finished setting the table.

When Uncle Ted arrived home, he was pleased to hear that Kay got a job.

"I guess it was worth it after all, that madcap junket of yours to Haiti. What does your job involve," he wanted to know.

She went into detail about cosmesis and how a frame can be selected to enhance or detract the shape of a face. Kay was surprised that he evoked any interest in her or what she planned to do, since he never had in the past. Talking and describing to him what her duties would be filled her with some excitement about what lay ahead in the new setting, the new job.

• • • •

The next morning Kay reported for work and she liked everything about her new duties, even to the first emergency call she handled.

"My contact lens is stuck to my eye and I can't get it unglued," was the plaintive cry at the other end of the phone. "What should I do?"

"Don't do anything," advised Kay. "Come to the office and Dr. Novak will aid you."

Dr. Novak himself was an exceptionally sympathetic

and understanding employer and health professional. But the contrast with patient care in Haiti was marked. The problems were different in scope.

When Dr. Novak emerged from his examining room with an attractive brunette, he introduced her.

"This is Mrs. Osborne. First bifocals." He winked at Kay.

"Did the doctor talk to you about the invisible bifocals," Kay asked Mrs. Osborne.

"That's exactly what I want. I don't want that telltale line that gives away my age. I've never worn glasses before, so this is all kind of new to me."

"Are you interested in metal or plastic frames or the newer rimless?"

"Perhaps you can suggest something. There are so many frames here I really don't know where to begin," the patient said, looking around the room.

"Why don't we step over to the frame bar and see what we can find for you. You have a long face," Kay said, studying the patient's physiognomy, "and I'd recommend a style with a low temple. This will break the line from the forehead to the chin. Here's what we call a plastic frame. Try it on for size." Kay scrutinized Mrs. Osborne. "That's a very good fit for you. Take a look at it yourself in the mirror over there."

"The shape is all right and it feels good, too, but the color is not for me. What is this color?"

"Celery."

"Doesn't this frame come in any other shade?"

"Yes, it does: tortoise shell, raspberry, and avocado."

"Let me try the tortoise shell." Mrs. Osborne returned to the mirror. "Oh yes, that's it," she said delightedly.

"I'm glad you're so easy to please," Kay said. "Would you like to step over to my desk now? I have to make some measurements. Your glasses will be ready in a week and I will give you a call when they come in."

The rest of the day Kay answered the phone, assisted

patients in frame selections and measured them, checked out jobs from the lab, and did repairs and adjustments in addition to bookkeeping.

At closing time, Dr. Novak came out of his office. "I'd like a few words with you, Kay, before you leave."

Kay flushed, apprehensive that she neglected to do something and hoped that any first day mistakes would be forgiven.

"You can relax, Kay. I'm not reprimanding you," he said. "I want you to know how pleased I am with your work, though it's only your first day."

"Thank you, Doctor."

As long as she worked, her thoughts didn't wander to anything or anyone else. Haiti became a dream that didn't exist. It was during the drive home to Middleville that she thought about Mac, much too often for her own good, she knew that. It was on the drive home, too, that she knew Haiti was not a dream, as the memory of her trip stirred up images she knew she'd never be able to forget.

. . . .

Kay fell easily into a routine of working, going home, preparing dinner, as if there had never been a disruption in her former lifestyle.

The bridesmaid gown, a gossamer creation in apricot, was delivered the following evening. Kay marveled at the perfect fit. The lines were quite becoming to her with its sweetheart neckline, tight bodice, and full flowing skirt. She was admiring it in her mirror when the phone rang downstairs.

"Uncle Ted, will you get that for me, please?"

Kay stood at the landing, curious to learn who the caller was. She heard her uncle's gruff, "Hello," in greeting.

"She's getting ready for the wedding," he said.

There followed a second of silence and Uncle Ted replied, "Jim Barlow is the groom. Good-bye."

"Uncle Ted, who was that?"

"He didn't say."

"Was there a message?"

"No. Probably not too important."

Mary Ellen called the next evening to find out about the gown.

"It's beautiful and fits well," Kay said.

"The color should be right for you, too. Do you think the neck is a trifle too bare?"

"What did you have in mind?" Kay asked.

"A single strand of pearls. If you don't have any, you can wear mine. How's the new job, by the way?"

"I like it."

"Before I forget, Kay, some of the opticians in the area are planning an old fashioned roller skating party. Would you like to come and get acquainted?"

"Thanks but no thanks, Mary Ellen, not this time."

"Don't stay home too much longer. You've got to get out and moving a little more."

"I suppose so."

"I'll be getting together with you for lunch one of these days, Kay, so take care till then."

. . . .

Two weeks elapsed and Kay felt she had been working for Dr. Novak forever. She was checking out some lenses in the lensmeter when the doctor entered the dispensing area.

"The Optic Fair will be held in Boston next week. How would you like to represent me?"

Shyly, Kay shook her head.

"No? I'm surprised. Most of my former employees jumped at a chance for a free all-expense trip like that."

"I've done enough traveling for awhile," Kay replied,

knowing full well this was a feeble excuse. What would she do in Boston anyway, sit and mope for Mac? What could she possibly say to him if she bumped into him at the Fair?

"I thought if you went," Dr. Novak said, "you'd come home with the news about the latest frame styles and the hottest tints we should feature."

"I think I'll sit this one out, Doctor, if you don't mind."

"Have it your own way."

As he retreated down the hall, she called out to him, "Please don't think I'm ungrateful for your offer. It's just," she groped for words, " that it's not a good time for me to leave town."

"I understand," he said, "you have obligations at home?"

"Yes, that's it."

A week later, Mary Ellen called and suggested the two of them meet for lunch on a Saturday to catch up on all the gossip.

They began their marathon talk session at a place halfway between Middleville and Hilldale. When they had exhausted all the news, Mary Ellen grew serious.

"Kay, I'm worried about you."

"Me? Why?"

"All you do is work, work, work. You don't have any time for the fun and recreation we used to share."

"You know how it is. By the time I get home at night, I'm tired, just plain weary. Then after I've made dinner, cleaned up the kitchen, read the paper, all I want to do is climb into bed and call it a day."

"But that's no life for you. You used to be a high spirited girl. What's happened to you?"

"Getting older and wiser, and chasing around doesn't seem that much important to me any more, nor does it appeal to me."

"You haven't even gotten back into circulation since your return from Haiti. A couple of fellows in town have asked me whether you're available for dating or what?"

"No thanks."

"Why not? You and I used to double date a long time ago, don't you remember?"

"That's it. That was a long time ago."

"Kay, listen to me. Do me a favor. Jim has a buddy who will be coming through this area, and Jim promised to fix him up with a date. Naturally, Jim thought of you right away. I think it's a super idea."

"Well, I don't. I'm sorry, Mary Ellen. I didn't mean to sound so abrupt." She reached out and touched her friend's hand. "It's just that blind dates never interested me in the past and I've been feeling so dragged out lately that I don't feel up to going out at all, period."

"That's it exactly. You feel so dragged out because all you do is work. Kay, one blind date won't hurt you. Besides, the guy is from out of town and you'll probably never see him again."

"Mary Ellen, I know you mean well, but I don't think I'm very good company for anyone these days."

"Baloney. Now you listen to me. You're going to go on a double date with us. Jim already spoke to his friend and set up the date."

"I guess I don't have much choice then, do I?"

"Are you mad at me?"

"No. How could I be? I know you're trying to help me."

Mary Ellen squeezed her hand. "That's great and I promise you'll have the time of your life. The date is for next Saturday."

"You don't waste much time, do you?" Kay quipped.

"Never mind, you promised. The four of us will have dinner at the Hi Jinx. We'll stay a little later for the dancing, too, and pick you up at 6:30." Mary Ellen looked at her watch. "I'm late as usual. Got to run. See you Saturday."

Kay realized she didn't even know her date's name, what he looked like, what kind of work he did. Nothing. She sighed. If things get deadly dull, Mary Ellen will keep everybody in stitches.

But as Saturday night approached, Kay looked with dread at the arranged blind date. Putting on an act was repugnant and too much of an effort. She had always been a lousy actress and couldn't pretend that something was when it wasn't.

She should have stuck to her guns about no dating, instead of caving in to Mary Ellen. She and Jim had a lot of friends and could have easily found another girl for this guy.

It was too late now. She'd have to go through with this charade.

On the night of her date, Kay wore the same outfit she had worn the first night she was in Haiti. Uncle Ted had gone to the Elks Club for his weekly game of poker and Kay was glad she was alone in the house while getting ready.

She finished applying a blusher to her cheeks, added a shade of pale pink to her lips, and clipped on her earrings when the doorbell rang.

"Just a moment," she called. She scurried about the small living room, fluffing up the pillows on the sofa, and straightening a couple of pictures over the fireplace. Then she opened the door. Her heart stopped.

"Hello, Kay," he said.

"Kay, I want you to meet a friend of mine," Jim said, right behind him. "Oh, have you met before?" he wisecracked. "Well, don't stand there, do something."

"No," Kay said to Mac. That's all she got to say as he crushed her in his arms, his lips hungrily seeking hers.

"How I've missed you, Kay, wondering why you left, where you went. No note, no trace, as if you vanished from the face of the earth. Only the Haitian print, left behind, as a reminder you had passed that way. Why, Kay, why?"

Her thoughts were a jumble. She didn't realize how much she had missed him and loved him until he walked through the door.

Then reason overtook her. She forgot for a moment why she had left Haiti so hurriedly. He was making a mockery of their relationship with his engagement and perhaps, marriage to Ruth.

She blinked back the tears, shook her head, pushed him away from her.

"How's Ruth?" she managed to ask.

"What are you worried about Ruth for?"

"Weren't you engaged to Ruth?"

"Never."

"She told me your engagement was going to be announced at the staff party."

"She was right about my engagement. It was going to be announced, except it was going to be to you. But you had to take off, like the creature of impulse that you are, without waiting for an explanation or asking for one."

"What else could I conclude?"

He wrapped his arms around her. "Dear, sweet Kay, I want you, need you, and love you." He nuzzled her neck. "Marry me, Kay."

The doorbell rang. "Say are you two lovebirds coming or what?" Jim asked. "We're waiting for you."

"Shall we?" Mac asked Kay. Their arms entwined around one another, they moved toward Jim's car.

On the way to the restaurant, neither Kay nor Mac spoke a word, their eyes seeking each other.

"It sure is quiet in the back seat," Jim said. "Mary Ellen, take a look behind you and see if they're still alive."

"They couldn't be more alive!" she reported.

. . . .

If someone had asked Kay what she had for dinner that night, she might be able to say it was food. That was all she knew. She was aware only of the man next to her, nothing else.

After they finished eating, Mary Ellen, rising from the table, a grin on her pixie face, leaned over confidentially. "You two don't mind being left alone, do you, while we work off those calories we stashed away?"

"Jim," Mary Ellen said, "do you think we were that lovesick when we started going with one another?"

"Worse," Jim said. "Come on, let's dance and leave them alone."

"You know, Kay," Mac said, "when I returned to the clinic that Wednesday from Port-au-Prince and found you gone, I was sure you had run off with Jim. I couldn't believe it. It didn't make any sense because you had told me that Biff had made you an offer."

"But I never said I accepted it, did I?"

"Ruth said you had left with Jim."

"How did she know?"

"She didn't, but since you left on the same day as Jim, what else could she conclude? There was no other logical explanation as to why, without as much as a word, you took off like that."

"After Ruth told me of her engagement to you," Kay said, "I knew I had to get out of your life."

"If only you had said something to me. When Ruth and I returned to Boston, we parted amicably. Ruth was only a friend, nothing more, ever. Regardless of any impression she might have given you, it has been you all the time, Kay.

"I don't know when I fell in love with you; whether it was at the airport when I first laid eyes on you or when I suddenly became incensed the night you had gone out with Jim; or when you went back to Nicole's house to retrieve her doll so she wouldn't be frightened. I missed you, Kay," he said.

"Aren't you two going to dance?" Mary Ellen said, as she and Jim returned to the table.

"For old times' sake?" Mac asked Kay.

How easily she fit in the curve of his arm and they glided across the floor.

"Happy?" he asked, looking down at her.

She nodded. "Very."

He placed his cheek next to hers, then pulled away. "I almost forgot. Biff sent me a copy of the brochure. Have you seen it?"

Kay shook her head.

"It's very effective. Too bad Biff thought there were other ways to make money. He's a fine photographer. Biff was arrested, so I heard. Jim told me you had helped him with the sting operation. Now I know why you were searching for something in my office and why you kept asking me about my surgery. Did you really think I was guilty?"

Kay felt her face grow warm.

"The only thing I'm guilty of is being in love with you, Kay. But getting back to the surgery—of course, I operated on patients in Port-au-Prince. Why not? After all, I was innocent of any charges against me in my malpractice suit, so why shouldn't I use my skills?"

"But when I asked you . . ." Kay began.

"I never said I did and I never said I didn't, remember?"

"Why didn't you give me an answer then?"

"Because I felt it was none of your business. I was just as suspicious of you as you were of me. I found the attaché case in your closet . . ."

"Which you appropriated," Kay said, smiling at his dismay.

"It belonged to me, my pet. Don't look so crushed. I forgive you."

"We never did get to Citadelle, did we?" asked Kay, anxious to divert the conversation to a more neutral topic.

"I was mad, mad as hell about that whole day," he said. "That was a day I couldn't forget for a long time."

"Neither could I," said Kay.

"I called your home the other day and when a man answered—was that your uncle?—I asked to speak to you. He said you were getting ready for the wedding rehearsal. Then when I asked who the groom was and found out it was Jim,

I was furious, furious that I had been made a fool of, and assumed you were the bride.

"I've been so tied up at the office since I returned from Haiti, I didn't have a chance to break away and try to find you. After that call, I knew I had to talk to Jim as soon as possible. I flew out here to . . ."

Kay placed a finger over his lips. The music had stopped and they returned to their table.

"What did you two decide?" Mary Ellen asked.

"How does a double wedding sound?" Mac asked.

"You mean I'm going to lose a bridesmaid," Mary Ellen wailed.

"But I'm going to gain a bride," Mac said, beaming at Kay.

The End